My Favorite Mistake

USA TODAY BESTSELLING AUTHOR
CLAUDIA BURGOA

Christine, this one is for you.
Thank you for your friendship and love.

"Love makes your soul crawl out from its hiding place."

-Vincent Van Gogh

Chapter One

Caspian

I SEALED my future the first time I put on a pair of ice skates.

I was three.

It wasn't until the age of five that I began playing organized hockey. My favorite thing in the world was when my father would take me to watch the San Jose Sharks. We had season tickets. Being one of eight children made it hard to have one-on-one time with him. His favorite sport was hockey, and lucky for me, I was the one out of all his kids who picked up the sport.

That was the way we bonded—until he died. Since then, I dedicated most of my free time to practice because I wanted to make him proud. I wanted to be a professional hockey player. When I'm on the ice, I feel him next to me.

Joel Spearman was a savvy businessman, a winemaker, but most of all, he was an extraordinary father. I was fifteen years old when he died. Each one of us coped differently.

Mom went into a deep depression.

My oldest brothers, who were twenty at the time, quit college and came home to take care of us. Aslan, Gatsby, and Lysander became our surrogate parents.

Fern, my older sister, became Mom's caregiver—and at times, she was our mother too. She was just sixteen.

Heathcliff, who was thirteen, spent more and more time between the pages of his books. I don't know what to call a guy who makes introverted people look like the life of the party. He's not dull. He's just…Heath.

Huxley and Cordelia, the youngest of the family, were eleven, and we all tried our best to ensure they didn't feel like the world was ending.

I was fifteen and spent most of the time on the ice or studying because my goal was to become the best professional hockey player. I wanted to make my father proud.

We survived, became a strong family, but we're all a little damaged on the inside.

I suppose this is how I became who I am today.

A hockey player, wine aficionado, cynic playboy—at least, that's the concept everyone has about me. It was a consequence of the perfect storm. Loss of a loved one, moving to another state and leaving my family behind, being drafted by one of the best hockey teams in the league. I had to pretend to be someone I was not.

At eighteen, I moved to Boston for college. I've been playing for the Vancouver Orcas for the past six years. I dedicate my life to making my father proud and staying close to him. Hockey was our thing, and I still share it with him.

I could say that I answer to no one, except Dawn Spearman —my mother. Once she learned to live with the grief of losing my father, she became what we like to call *Helicopter Dawn*. I adore the lady, but when she gets overbearing I can't handle her.

We try to remain close to each other but for me it's almost impossible.

During my off-season, I live in Paradise Bay and spend my time helping my brother Lysander in the vineyard. And no, I don't live with my mother. She has a lovely home with eight bedrooms and plenty of room to stay away from each other—in theory. Dawn is always on my case. I adore my mother, but I'm too old to be micromanaged by her.

I'm supposed to take a break and rest. Instead, I'm working in the wine tasting room, repairing things around the vineyard, or being Lysander's bitch. That's what my brother calls me. It's a pain in the ass to have three older brothers who think they rule us all.

"We need to replace the fence on the west side," Lysander announces as he enters the tasting room.

"You don't expect me to do that, do you?"

He smirks.

The fucker smirks.

"Listen, I'll pay for any repairs. Vacation time is almost over, and you know what happens after that?"

"Your chariot turns back into a pumpkin, and your peasant clothes become a hockey jersey?"

I roll my eyes.

He makes some sound as if I'm annoying him. "Where is your sense of humor?"

"I lost it a couple of weeks ago when I almost broke my leg," I growl.

"It's not my fault you don't know how to climb a ladder."

"On Monday, I'll hire a company to build you a new fence, cheapskate."

"Hey, don't call me names. I'm trying to find things for you to do around the vineyard. This is me doing you a favor. We have plenty of money to pay for that."

I glare at him. "Stop"—I draw air quotes—"doing me any favors. I can manage without your help."

"You're in a mood. Do you know what you need?"

"Scotch, cognac…who knows?"

He shakes his head. "You need to get laid. When was the last time you did it?" He rubs his neck, pretending that he's thinking. "Once you were in the playoffs, you stopped having sex. If we add the few weeks you've been here and count that time when Cory cockblocked you because you tried to sleep with her friend…six months?"

"Are you keeping track of my dating life?"

He scoffs, quirking an eyebrow. "Do you date?"

I cock my head. An unapologetic smile spreads across my face. "I like to call it that, even if it doesn't last long."

He shakes his head. "You're full of shit."

That I am. Everyone swears that hockey players get tail all the time. Puck bunnies are easy to score. I let everyone believe that I sleep around with randos every night. I don't. When I find a woman intriguing enough to share a meal with, I might take her to my room or follow her to her apartment. But it doesn't happen often.

It's hard to find a woman interested in getting to know me. They all want to sleep with Caspian "Cassie" Spearman. The best forward in the conference. In college, I couldn't get enough of the attention, but as I grew older, the novelty disappeared.

Maybe that's why I choose to stick around in the vineyard during the off-season instead of joining my teammates. They're traveling around the world, partying with their girlfriends—or meeting a different chick every single night.

"So other than having to build a new fence, what else do you have for me?"

"When are you leaving?"

"You have one week left to have fun with me. Next Monday I

have to be in Vancouver. We get to learn the fate of the club." My smile doesn't drop, but my hands get clammy just thinking about the meaning of that last sentence.

Last year, Mills Aldridge bought the team. We don't know if he did it to spite the owners who released him from his contract or…well, there hasn't been an explanation. Since then, everyone has been talking about the future of the team. We might move to the East Coast before the season starts or…who knows.

There are two things I'm afraid of. One is that he might move the team so far it would be impossible to visit my family as often as I do. The second is that they'll trade me to another team. It's bound to happen, but I don't like the idea of leaving the people I've been with since my career started.

Mills Aldridge and I used to get along, but since they cut him from the team, I lost track of him, and well…it'd be strange to call and ask about my future on the team. The next week is going to be agonizing. My throat grows tight as the day I have to be back in Vancouver comes closer.

I should find a distraction. Maybe Lysander is onto something. I should get laid. It's been a long time. Too long.

But how can I find someone when Paradise Bay has no more than two thousand people and way too many people in San Francisco recognize me?

Chapter Two

Rys

MOM ALWAYS WARNED me about men.

I think the first time it happened was when I was five—after my parents' divorce. Dad is a decent father. I can't say anything about being a husband. Once I started college, Mom sent me the occasional text: *Stay away from college boys.* Or another random one would be: *They only want you for your body.*

One way or another, she always found a way to remind me

that I was in school to learn, not to drink or sleep my way through the entire fraternity. My younger sister, who is an irreverent brat, asked her which fraternity, so I could go to the others. That's Milly, my sister, always upsetting our mother with her nonsense. And yes, our names are ridiculous: Polly and Milly. It's a lot better than Polaris and Millenya. Our names are grounds to accuse our parents of child abuse.

It's been a year since I graduated from veterinary school, yet she's still sending me texts with the same boring warnings.

My sister, whose other superpower is being passive-aggressive, waited until her boyfriend knocked her up to introduce him to Mom as the guy she had just met at a bar. All lies. Ernest and Milly have been together since college and had lived together for five years before my cute nephew came into the world. I'm guessing it's some kind of retribution for all the years Mom's been trying to convince us to stay away from men, which is why I kept Ernest a secret from our mother too.

Have I listened to her?

No, but I don't date that much. It's not for the lack of trying. I've been too busy.

Vet school was hectic. During the last year of school, I found a great guy who ghosted me when I told him I had to move to Oregon for my internship. Kevin couldn't even tell me it was over. In my personal experience, there are five kinds of men I need to stay away from.

The liar, the player, the selfish, the controlling, and the emotionally unavailable.

You'd think that I'd stay away from them, but unfortunately I don't realize they're in those categories until it's too late.

Way too late.

While working on my internship in Baker's Creek, I didn't date anyone. It wasn't because there weren't any candidates, but my boss warned me about the town's size and the gossip. The queen bees of that town post everything on social media. I stayed off their radar for an entire year. That and graduating from vet school are my proudest achievements from the past couple of years.

While working there, I made a few friends, like Avery Sanders, who lives full-time in New York City but often visits her family. There are times when we agree to meet somewhere in the country. Like this weekend we decided to drink our way through the northern part of California to celebrate my new job. Yesterday we visited five vineyards in Napa Valley. Today, we're visiting Paradise Bay. Our first stop was the spa, and we had lunch at a small Italian place called Trattoria Dionisia.

We spend about an hour learning how to pronounce the restaurant's name and some basic Italian. The servers recommend we visit Paradise Bay Winery. They have a great selection of wine, and their tasting room is delightful. If we arrive around four, they serve appetizers for the visitors.

Everything sounds lovely until Avery's best friend, Benedict Farrow, catches up with us. Can this guy stop ruining our girls' weekends? Today's excuse: I was in Baker's Creek helping your brother Hayes with the clinic, and it seemed like a good idea to come and visit you.

That's a nine-hour drive or a two-hour flight. This guy is in love with my friend, but Avery rolls her eyes and dismisses me when I point out the obvious.

So, here I am, playing the third wheel on our way to a gorgeous vineyard, hoping that there's someone I can at least talk to for the next thirty minutes—or however long the tasting lasts. Can I just buy a few bottles and head back to my hotel room? Oh no, wait. Our room is in San Francisco, and Avery is the one who has the car keys. I should leave the *friends* stranded in wine country.

But then what am I supposed to do?

This weekend is all about enjoying fermented grapes and the gorgeous landscapes these lands offer us. We park the car outside the vineyard, walking past the open black iron gate. There's a clear lake in the middle of the property, surrounded on three sides by the land where the grapes grow, and the other has a gorgeous patio, a gazebo, and a majestic house.

"I think I'm in love," Avery says as we take in the entire scenery. "This is one of the best vineyards I've seen—including the ones in France."

"It's beautiful," I say, a little jealous that she's been to France.

My parents worked hard to provide us with a good education, clothing, and the essentials. My vacations were to my grandparents' house. Maternal for the summer, paternal for the winter holidays.

"We should go to Europe. When do you think you can take some vacation?"

I shrug. Sometimes, my friend forgets that we come from different backgrounds. Though she has a job and works as hard as me, she also has a trust fund and a father who is one of the wealthiest men in the world. Me… "Well, I start my new job in a week. Meaning, I don't have time off for a year or so."

"We'll figure out something. I can talk to Leyla. She might let you off the hook for a few days."

Her sister-in-law is my boss, and though I love Avery to pieces, I have to remind her of my cardinal rule. "We don't mix our friendship with my job, remember."

She gives me an apologetic look. "Sorry."

"Let's go drink some wine," I say, brushing away that conversation and turning to Benedict. "You know what you should do?"

"I'm afraid of what you're going to suggest."

I smile sweetly. "Oh, I was going to say be our designated driver since you showed up late for the party."

He looks at me for a second and shakes his head. I'm not sure what that means. "Why don't we head to the wine tasting room?"

We follow the signs to what looks like a gorgeous rustic cabin. There's a tall, handsome guy leaving the cabin. He spots us and grins. "I didn't know you were coming," the man says, making his way toward us.

Who is he talking to?

"Well, my friends planned on coming to visit you, and I wanted to make sure you'd treat them right."

The guy shakes hands with Benedict and hugs him. "How have you been?"

"Busy, being a doctor is not as easy as they make you believe in medical school," he laughs. "Is Heath in San Fran, or did you put him to work?"

"He avoids working at the vineyard, which is why he never tells me his schedule. What brings you here?"

Benedict waves a hand toward us. "As I mentioned, my friends are here to visit the vineyard. Avery, Rys, meet Lysander. He's one of the owners and the manager of this vineyard."

Lysander nods. "It's nice meeting you, ladies. Let me guess." He points at Avery. "You like sweet wines."

She shakes her head. "You're going to be wrong if you're trying to decide what I like. Dad trained me to enjoy every type of wine. Do I have a preference? It depends on my mood."

He looks at me. "What about you?"

"I drank wine in a box during college. At this point, anything will do," I answer.

He smirks. "Cas is going to have fun serving them."

Benedict looks toward the tasting room. "Caspian is in today?"

"Yep, why don't you let them join him, and you help me in the lab. I'm trying to decide if cider is in the future of Paradise Bay Winery."

Benedict looks at us. "You guys okay if I leave?"

"Please, like I need you while I'm drinking wine. We'll be perfectly fine," Avery says, grabbing my hand and pulling me toward the tasting room.

I'm curious by nature, and I *have* to know how Benedict knows these people. Is that why he joined us? "So…Benedict and this Lysander guy are related or something? He seems to know them pretty well."

Avery's green eyes crinkle. "Of course he does. I'm pretty

sure Ben's mission in life is to meet all seven billion people living on the planet before the age of fifty. He's a friendly person."

She is right. I might not be a fan of him because he's always the third wheel—and makes me feel like I imposed—but that's probably an internal issue I have to work on.

The owner is handsome. Tall, a towering six foot three, with dark eyes and a flashy smile. The man behind the counter in the tasting room is just as tall but with piercing grayish eyes and a mischievous smirk that says, *I'm-going-to-fuck-you-and-you'll-never-forget-me.*

"Hello, ladies." The baritone tone of his voice sends my pulse to an abnormal speed.

"Hi," Avery, who's the extroverted one of the two of us, greets him. "Is the place usually empty on Saturdays?"

"It is during the air balloon festival in Craigtown," he answers, and his voice continues to make my knees weak. "If you ask me, we shouldn't be open today, but what do I know, I'm just the server."

I giggle at his poorly delivered joke.

I giggle.

That's not me.

His suave smile widens, and he says, "What would you like to try today? We have a fine selection of wine that goes from dry and spicy to sweet and tangy."

I'll drink you, I want to say because it's been a long time since I've been with a guy.

Wouldn't it be nice to break the dry spell with someone like him? I bet he knows his way around the female body.

Avery reaches for her phone, which is in her back pocket, and sighs.

"Is it your brothers?"

She shakes her head. "No. It's Ben. He needs me to taste the best cider in the world." She turns to look at me. "Do you want to come?"

"My wine is a lot better than my brother's crappy cider. You should stick around," he says with a raspy voice that almost makes me come.

If anything, I should record his voice and make it my ringtone.

Avery looks at me expectantly. "Why don't I stay? If I get drunk enough, I might forget that I'm the third wheel."

She glares at me. "You're insane. I'll be back soon, promise."

I watch her leave the tasting room, and once the door closes, I hear tall-dark-and-fuckable say, "Well, it's just you and me. This might get interesting." He winks at me. "What do you want to taste?"

You?

I stare at him, fidgeting my lips between my teeth.

Chapter Three

Caspian

I MIGHT HAVE FOUND a good reason not to pack my shit and leave.

I hate my brother, but if things work out, I'll keep him alive for another year or so.

Hate might be too strong of a word, but I'm not a fan of him right now. As I always say, he gets a kick out of using my time as if he owns it. Lysander keeps the tasting hours open when I'm around just to fuck with me. No one believes me, but he does.

I was tempted to leave my post and take a swim until the two gorgeous women burst into the tasting room. Both are pretty, but I prefer petite, curvy, shy girls.

This one has long, dark luscious hair, brown doe eyes, and her lips are pouty—kissable.

I want to press my mouth to hers and taste them. She might have come here to drink a glass of Chardonnay, but I'm willing to give her a lot more if she accepts it.

Reaching for the glasses, I ask, "What's your poison?"

"What do you guys grow?"

With that siren voice, my cock is the only thing growing right now—and getting so fucking hard. I clear my throat, wondering why she's affecting me so much. I'm usually around women who wear fewer clothes than she is, and I don't react the way I'm responding to her. I want to remind myself that chemistry only lasts for so long and that once she recognizes me, the shy act will disappear.

She's staring at me expectantly.

"Grapes," I answer with a sly smile on my face.

"Color me surprised. For a moment, I believed you were growing weed and hay." She sits on the barstool across from me. "I was asking the type of grapes. Some vineyards only grow one kind. You seem to have enough land to have at least two or three. The place is beautiful, by the way."

"Thank you. My father chose it to create one of the best wineries in the world. I don't know if we've accomplished that, but we're working on it."

She stares at me. "As I mentioned, it's a great place. What do you produce?"

"I'll be honest with you, darling," I say, leaning closer to her. "My jam is to make you drink and sell you lots of wine cases. Whatever is growing outside isn't my territory."

She smiles. "Meaning they don't pay you enough to deal with more than what's around this room?"

"They don't pay me shit," I clarify. "I spend my PTO working for them. Are you ready for your first taste? I'll give you our boldest and our sweetest wines, and we can go from there."

I grab a bottle of Syrah and then a bottle of Riesling. I pour them into different glasses.

I push the red wine first. "This is our Syrah from two thousand and five. Dad added a note not to open it until two thousand nineteen. We don't know his reasoning, but this bold wine is one of the strongest. The range of flavors—the dark fruits, peppers, notes of herbs, and smoke—pair perfectly with a steak."

She sips it and scrunches her nose. "I'm a vegetarian."

Well, there goes my idea to invite her to the guesthouse and grill a couple of steaks.

"The wine is nice, but your pickup line needs a lot of work," she mumbles, drinking the dark liquid slowly.

I rest my arms on the counter and lean forward. "It wasn't a pickup line."

"You're wasting your time with me."

"Why?"

She waves her hand around her hair. "The alarms are sounding. You're either a player, a liar, emotionally unavailable, or something like that."

"What gives you that idea?"

"You're too pretty."

I laugh. "Pretty?"

"Sure, look at you."

I humor her and glance at myself as if I'm studying every inch of my body. "So, you like what you see?"

She flicks her wrist from left to right a couple of times. "It's fine. If you're into the whole shallow exterior."

"Every relationship begins with attraction. If you're not attracted, nothing is going to happen with the other person no matter what he does."

She gives me a skeptical look. "What happens to those who are friends for years, and slowly begin to fall in love?"

"The guy is either a coward or an idiot."

"So, once you're attracted to someone, you fall in love, and then what happens?"

"Well, it's not that easy."

She snorts. "You have a degree in Theoretical Bullshit, don't you?"

I laugh. She might be shy, but she's funny once she gets comfortable. I like that.

"No, but I'll look into that degree. It might come in handy. What I'm saying is that I'm not attracted to just anyone. Maybe it's because I don't have the chance to meet beautiful women who intrigue me." I pause, leaning closer before saying, "Like you."

"Like me?"

"I don't know much about you, but from the moment you walked in, I've wanted to learn more. That doesn't happen to me often."

"What's the point? I'll be leaving in twenty minutes, and you'll forget I existed."

"We could make this an unforgettable evening. I'll invite you to my house. We'll grill some eggplants—"

"Let me stop you before you begin a disturbing analogy of your elongated cock being seared by my velvety—"

"Whoa, I meant eggplant. You just said you're a vegetarian."

I try not to laugh, but her face turns slightly red and I can't help myself.

"Oh...I—" She's all flustered and cute.

"I take it you've been approached by douches who don't care to get to know you before they're offering more than a kiss."

"Not personally. I have friends who tell me stories. I've been out of the dating scene for years."

Fuck, so she's married. I'm wasting my time and hitting on another guy's woman. That's not my style. "I'm sorry if I came on too strong. Was your husband the guy with Lysander?"

"What, Benedict Farrow?" She makes a pinched expression. "Eww, no, thank you."

"Ben is here?"

"You know Benedict?"

"That kid went to college and med school with my younger brother. If he's with Lysander, he's not going to leave the house for at least a week or so."

"Why do you say that?"

"He's like family, and Lysander treats family like his employees. We—family—need to do something to help the vineyard. I don't think you're leaving for a couple of days."

When I deliver the news, she gawks at me. "But I need to be at my new job on Monday."

"We'll make sure that you arrive at your destination. In the meantime, we can close this place and head to the store for some supplies."

"Supplies?"

"Do you always repeat what others tell you?"

She nods, tapping her ear. "I have auditory processing disorder. Sometimes, I hear weird things, but I'm able to fix them to make sense. Other times, I repeat the word to ensure that I got it right. It's a disability that sucks sometimes. There are songs—mostly children's songs—that I only hear the word fuck repeated over and over again. It's horrifying."

My youngest brother, Huxley, has ADHD. Living with disabilities is complicated. "I didn't mean to embarrass you."

"Oh, you didn't…well, it's horrifying that people call me out on my habit. Then, if I explain why I do it, it gets worse. They talk slowly, making me feel like an idiot. This is why I like to work with animals instead of dealing with people."

"Well, I promise never to bring it back up." I cross my heart with my index finger. "Ready to ditch this joint?"

"I shouldn't."

"Do you have any other place to go?"

"Let's begin with: I don't know you."

I grab her delicate hand and kiss her knuckles. "I'm Caspian, but my family and friends call me Cas. You are?"

She swallows, looking at my hand and then my lips. "Rys," she whispers.

"Well, Rys. I propose we take a break from real life. We'll make this day unforgettable. By Monday, we'll walk back into our lives. What do you think?"

She snatches her hand away from my grip, and while staring at it, she asks, "Is that another pickup line?"

"Nope. I'm telling you my plan."

"Are there any other options?"

"Lysander can bore you to tears while he gives you an entire class on how to make cider, and he also adds chemistry terms to that shit."

"It'd be like organic chemistry. I did well in that class."

I gasp dramatically. "You're some sort of scientist?"

She nods. "Yep. Is that a problem? Let me guess, you were a jock."

I shrug. "People assume that I am, but I really didn't belong to any specific group. I'm my own person. So, what do you say? Do you want to spend the rest of the day with me?"

Chapter Four

Rys

THIS IS like walking willingly to a torture chamber.

I know what's going to happen inside. I only have a few seconds left before the doors close, and I have to stay.

But why would I leave?

It's been a long time since I've been around a guy who isn't looking for me because I can treat their pets. He genuinely wants to spend the rest of the evening with me.

Is it a good idea?

No.

Should I look for the exit?

Yes.

What are my options? Join Avery and… I hate Benedict. Why did he have to drag Avery to try cider? I usually don't mind when they leave me behind. I'm a loner, but if anything happens with this guy, I'll blame him for the rest of my life.

I look at his eyes. My entire body rattles as they meet with mine. The zing that spread through my body when he kissed me still travels around at a million miles per hour. I don't recall the last time I felt that way. It's been a long time. Too long since my heart pitter-pattered for a man. Leaving might be the best idea. I've no idea where I'd go, but if I stay with him and do something stupid…

What can happen?

You'll be living in Oregon, and you'll never cross paths with him. This is the first time a good-looking stranger is offering me… what is he offering me? Getting away from reality.

I can handle it, can't I?

"Don't make me regret it," I warn him.

We go to a small store for supplies. When he's about to grab a big eggplant, I confess the truth. I'm not a vegetarian, but I avoid pork, red meat, and chicken as much as possible—unless it's chicken nuggets. I love breaded poultry. Who am I kidding? I just love bread and pastries.

He picks up ingredients to make pasta, salad, and he buys chocolate cake for dessert. "It's the best in town," he assures me.

"With a population of two hundred people, of course, it's the best."

"We're almost two thousand residents and counting," he says, serving me with a proud smile.

"Are you trying to get me drunk?" I ask as I hold my third glass of the day. This time I'm drinking a Pinot Grigio. He says it has a delicate citrus flavor (lime water, orange zest), pomaceous fruits (apple skin, pear sauce), and white floral notes. It's light compared to the Malbec I drank before. They're all delicious, but he's trying to train my palate.

It's going to take more than one evening, but I'm humoring him.

"The wine from Paradise Bay doesn't get you drunk. It makes you happy."

I lift one of the bottles of wine, reading the label. "Is that the slogan? Because you might've forgotten to add it in the design."

He chuckles and reaches for the cutting board. "It was my father's mantra."

"He sounds pretty passionate about his wine."

"He was…" There's a long silence.

I reach out for his hand and squeeze it. "I'm sorry."

"It's been almost fourteen years, but it still hurts. He was the foundation of our family."

"Why don't I help you?" I offer since I don't know how to fill the silence. If I knew him better, I could say the right words, but right now…

"Sure, you can rinse the vegetables. It'll take us less time to cook. The sky is clear. We could eat out," he offers.

Eating outside sounds like a dream. I'm sure it's not France, but the place is just as romantic, isn't it? "Why don't you tell me about your family while we prepare the food?"

"You don't want me to bore you. Why don't you tell me about your new job?"

He doesn't have to ask me twice. As he shows me his outstanding skills in the kitchen while sautéing the tomatoes, boiling the pasta, and preparing the pesto from scratch, I tell him about my passion.

Animals.

"Why choose studying in Colorado and moving to the West Coast?"

"I went on a scholarship. My boss gives three full rides every year to those who show potential. In exchange, we have to work for her for at least five years. I did my internship in one of her animal hospitals."

He stops chopping the onions. His gray, penetrating eyes stare at me with anticipation. I don't know what to tell him. Will he care to learn more about me?

"What about you?"

He goes back to prepping his food. "I don't save animals or handle furry creatures who lick my face. It's a lot about repetition and practice."

"You don't seem excited."

"I like it. Not many find it as intriguing as I do."

"If I were an actuary, I'd be as cryptic as you are."

He's not looking at me, but I can see his smile. "You caught me there. It's all about statistics and analyzing what's best for the team."

"Would you quit to dedicate your time to the vineyard?"

"This is Lysander's territory now. I don't know if he'd let any of us manage it along with him." He shrugs.

"How many siblings do you have?"

He tells me what it was like to grow up in a house with seven other siblings. As I hear how they spent their summers helping their father with the vineyard and swimming in the pool or the lake, I'm transported to the days when Milly and I were children.

I don't think we ever had that much fun. Mom always had something important to do, and we were stuck at home doing chores. Everything was about the next room we had to clean or the patio to be swept several times a week—it was dirty.

This isn't the conversation I planned to have with a stranger during our escape-from-reality day, but we end up discussing his seven brothers and sisters and my only sister. This isn't exactly what I planned on doing when Avery proposed we go wine dining, but I'm enjoying it a lot. I'm just waiting for that text that tells me it's over and we're heading back to San Francisco.

Chapter Five

Caspian

WE SPEARMANS TEND to gather strays and adopt them as part of our family. We did that with Benedict Farrow. Since he's like a little brother, it's easy to text him something like: *I'm going to be entertaining your friend. Make sure to disappear for a day or two.*

Did I get a warning back?

Of course. He told me not to be a fucking asshole to Rys— she's not a fan of his.

That intrigues me since Ben is the friendliest person on the planet. But he's a secondary character in this escapade, so I don't even bother to ask Rys what her deal is with Benedict. We spend the afternoon on the veranda just outside the master bedroom of the guesthouse. I'm glad Mom went on a retreat with my aunts. No one will interrupt us tonight.

"If I ever retire, I'll move to a place like this," she says, drinking some water.

She stopped accepting wine after the third glass. It's a shame because our wines are some of the best in the world. But it's also good because if anything happens between us, I want her sober.

"You're welcome to visit," I offer.

"This town would be perfect if there's a small hotel around."

"Where are you staying?"

She checks her watch and then her phone. "In San Francisco. We didn't find any rooms available around the area—"

I interrupt her. "It's festival season. The next time you want to come, call the vineyard. Someone will be able to tell you what's happening around town."

She nods, and I finally dare to ask about the small tattoo she has on the inside of her left arm. "Is that a constellation?"

Rys stares at her ink and sighs. "It's Ursa Minor."

"What's the story?"

"Do I have to have a reason?"

"There are three reasons a person gets a tattoo. They're drunk, they're sad, or they're in love."

"In love?"

"You could be in love with the idea of something, not necessarily a person. Which one is it?"

She moves the pendant that she's wearing. It's a P.

"Was his name Peter, Paul, Princeton…"

"Ha, it's not a guy. My name is…" Her voice trails off. "It's not important."

"Your name starts with a P, and the constellation has to do with it?"

She nods after a couple of seconds. "My name is Polaris Vega

—I'm named after Ursa Minor. My parents call me Polly, but I use Rys."

"That's a beautiful name and a great reason to have a tattoo."

"So how many tattoos do you have because you were…what was it?"

I laugh. "A few of them were done because I was sad." I pull up my shirt and show her the black and white milky way tattoo on my chest, which also has the date when Dad died.

She traces it, and I shiver. "This is beautiful and meaningful."

It is the only non-stupid tattoo I have and the tenderness in her eyes makes me take her into my arms and kiss her.

Our lips meet, and then I pull her closer, embracing her into a tight hug. Our tongues intertwine.

I breathe into the kiss I've wanted to give her since we were in the tasting room. She meets my passion with the same energy and desperation.

Her lips are so soft, her body so perfect, and I wish I had the time to meet her soul.

For one perfect moment, we're connected, two heartbeats intertwined. She's a cyclone of stardust. A cosmic force that's been pulling me to her since she arrived at Paradise Bay Winery.

I want her.

I just don't think I'll be able to keep her.

Chapter Six

Rys

THIS IS either the best night of my life or the biggest mistake I've ever made. When Avery sent me a text telling me that she had to stay with Benedict, I almost cursed at her, but how could I when she left me with a hot guy.

Well, he's not a bartender, but an actuary—a numbers guy. I love intelligent men who aren't afraid to be vulnerable. He might be over six feet tall, muscly, and as handsome as Liam

Hemsworth or Harry Styles, but the guy is soft on the inside. When he showed me the tattoo in honor of his father, I wanted to console him. I couldn't help but touch him.

And then…we kissed.

I don't know who started the kiss, but it was almost impossible to end it. He kisses me with the same passion as he speaks about his family. Mostly his dad.

Is this guy for real?

He might be a figment of my imagination, and instead of being in the master bedroom of the guesthouse, I'm on the floor of the tasting room, extremely drunk. I hope that's not the case because I want to finish this perfect night making love under the blanket of stars. This kiss is so powerful.

A lightning strike.

This is gravity binding us the way it does with the earth and the sun.

The collision of two stars.

A supernova being born.

This is Polaris illuminating the entire galaxy as it's about to explode. I've never felt anything like being sucked into something this strong—and it's just a kiss.

His lips are soft, firm, commanding.

He is in charge of us until he suddenly stops. "We don't have to do anything," he mumbles.

"But do we want to?"

That spark in his eyes burns my soul. How is it that I'm so turned on by him?

"We can do whatever we want," I say. "We're two consenting adults, aren't we?"

He begins to undress me slowly—first my blouse, then my leggings. He slides down the straps of my white bra, and I regret putting on cotton undergarments today.

He unveils my breasts. "You're beautiful," he whispers in awe.

"What do you have?" I ask, tugging his black Paradise Bay t-shirt.

I open my mouth wide. The sight is quite spectacular. Never before have I seen someone as handsome and sculpted like marble—a sexy mass of muscles and strength.

He's delicious. I touch the lines of his flat stomach, running them down until I unfasten his pants. My mouth waters as I stare at him, his heavily aroused erection. I want to touch him, grip him, and suck his engorged head. Before I can do anything, he pulls me into his arms and wraps them around me.

My hands slip around his back. "This night is going to be unforgettable," he promises.

He kisses me with such intensity I feel like I'm on fire. We get caught up in the heat. He pulls me into the lounge chair, lowering himself over me. I feel the hot wisp of his breath against my throat. I shiver with pleasure as he nibbles my skin. First along my neck, then my tits.

I push my hips up, seeking some friction, a way to relieve the ache between my legs, but nothing works.

His mouth is at my breast.

His tongue tracing circles until the tip hardens.

He repeats the same with my other one. He begins to lap faster and tug harder until I start moaning.

"Don't tease me," I beg him. And I'm not even sure what I want, for him to bring me to my knees or to have him inside.

I grip his shoulders when his fingers tease along the insides of my thighs, padding his way up to the middle of my body where he moves the thin fabric of my panties. I cry out and lift my hips when his thumb caresses my slit. He lowers my panties with his teeth and then pushes them down with his hand.

"Are you sure you want this?" he asks just as I'm on the edge and about to fall into a powerful orgasm.

"Please. I want it as much as you do."

He flashes me an assured smile as he moves his body back up and spreads my legs wider.

One second his face is between my legs, and the next, his tongue slides over my clit, slippery, wet, long, and hot.

Every nerve in my body awakens. He does it again, pressing

hard and moving slowly. The feeling is too much, overwhelming, and wonderful.

Suddenly, it's all too much.

His mouth.

His fingers.

His wild lips sucking me.

Those teeth, nibbling me. And the tongue sliding from my clit to my back hole. My blood runs hot. My cells vibrate with pleasure.

I'm tied into knots.

I'm desperate.

The thundering of my heart matches the rhythm of his mouth. My eyelids become heavy.

I'm close.

So close.

I want him inside me. But before I can speak, everything goes dark for a second, it's the prelude before the entire universe explodes and the sparks illuminate the horizon.

"I need you to fill me." It's the desire to have him inside me speaking. The lust. I want him to claim me. To brand me.

After covering his cock with a condom, he mounts the chair and lowers his body on top of mine. His eyes find mine.

I can't get enough of him.

His smile, those bright gray eyes.

Something about him feels perfect. He kisses me, and as I taste myself, I become erotically aroused.

Pleasure surges and buzzes with each flick of his tongue inside my mouth. Finally, one of his knees parts my legs. My body goes still when I feel him pressing himself slowly against my entrance.

I love the way his thickness fills me, easing himself slowly, making me tremble. I clutch his shoulders, my nails denting his skin. He's too big, and the deeper he goes, the more I want.

He moves gently, pulling slowly, thrusting at the same pace. It's a different rhythm, erotic, even sexy. The same way he kisses me. I want this fast and lift my hips, urging speed. I want it harder, faster. He doesn't budge. With one hand, he pins my hip down.

"I want us to enjoy our first time. Just feel it. All of us."

It's hard to surrender the control, but I let him lead. I enjoy the sweet thrusting and pulling. It's slow but continues, and it pushes me to the highest place I've ever climbed, and then in one instant, I explode into stardust, and I feel it as our particles combine. He rides my orgasm and plunges himself faster and harder until he finds his release and moans.

He collapses, his chin resting on my shoulder. "I could be doing this forever. Worshiping you."

And I want that so much, but I know it's an impossible dream.

Chapter Seven

Caspian

IT'S AROUND six in the morning when I wake up after a long night making love to Rys. I feel her next to me. She's such a beautiful woman, and I wish I could keep seeing her, but long-distance relationships are impossible. More so with my line of work. I've seen it all, jealous girlfriends, divorces because some of the players can't keep their dicks where they belong...what brings her into my life?

She's unique and makes me want to be with her forever. Her head rests on my bicep, her lengthy hair tied into a messy bun. I enjoy the sight because tomorrow morning she'll go on with her life and so will I.

My favorite night might become the best memory of my life.

Chapter Eight

Rys

IT WAS SEX.

Just sex.

Nothing but a fun, perfect night with a hot, so-out-of-my-league stranger.

He might say he's a boring actuary—nothing was boring about him.

He's hiding something.

Is he emotionally unavailable?

All I know is Caspian is a man who loves his family. He's probably a hot-as-hell, womanizing playboy.

I won't deny that I liked him.

Talking to Caspian was…different. I can't exactly define what happened between us. Chemistry, lust, loneliness. It was the perfect storm. The stars aligned, and the world stopped so we could have *just*…well, a weekend.

Staying overnight and spending part of Sunday with him doesn't say one-night stand, does it?

This thing between us was strange, explosive, and maybe unforgettable.

My stomach knots as I imagine what'll happen if I become addicted to his kisses after today.

It won't happen, I assure myself.

I'll never understand why I made him the exception to the rule. But I know it's over. By the time I reach the airport, Caspian will be nothing but a memory.

The driver he hired takes me to a small airport in wine country. There's a jet waiting for me. He asked me to call him when I got home, but I've already erased his number. It's a private flight, he'll know when I land. That's enough, isn't it?

This should end now, which is why I didn't offer my number. It's best if we cut all communication between us from the root. I can claim that I switched phones, and he…well, I'm sure he won't even remember who I was by the time he's sleeping with the next woman who crosses his path.

But can I do the same, forget all about him? I touch my lips, wondering if the heat will diminish soon.

It will, right?

Chapter Nine

Caspian

ALMOST THREE YEARS later

I'm in love.

Those who don't believe in love at first sight haven't met the most beautiful girl in the world. Soleil Roux Spearman.

"I'm your favorite uncle in the entire world," I whisper, cradling the pink bundle close to my chest.

"Get in line," Gatsby, one of my older brothers and the proud father of my first niece, says.

"Am I the last one meeting her?" I glance at him for a quick second, though it's hard to stop staring at his beautiful baby. How someone so obnoxious could create a miracle like Soleil is beyond me.

"Lysander called dibs on most favorite. He paid well for it. You might need to bribe us to move the needle in your favor."

If I wasn't carrying his daughter, I'd be flipping him the finger. Asshole.

"Stop teasing your brothers," Maia chides him. "We'll teach her not to pick favorites. He's just giving you a hard time, as he did with the rest."

I focus on my sister-in-law. "How are you feeling, Maia?"

She smiles, staring at the pink bundle in my arms. "Happy, but tired. Pushing her out was…well, not how I expected to start my day. She decided it was okay to arrive two weeks early."

Though the beautiful girl I hold sleeps soundly, I whisper, "You're as impatient as your father."

"Sure, blame me. My adorable wife is ten times more restless than I am. Our Little Sun takes after her."

I arch an eyebrow. Little Sun? *Why? What does that mean?*

He calls his wife Little Blue since her middle name is Azul. I need to know why we're calling this beauty *Little Sun.* "Explain?"

"Soleil means sun in French," he answers. "We tried to pick a name close to Maia—she's a little star too. If it was a boy, we were going to call him Rigel Joel. Maybe the next one?"

I don't know how to feel about him naming his son Joel. Should I call dibs on Dad's name? Maybe as a family we should discuss who gets to use it. I want to preserve his name, just as we've maintained his legacy. But is it fair to name a child after Joel Spearman?

Those are big shoes to fill, and…well, I stop because there's no point on thinking about my future children.

Fortunately, Maia interrupts all my thoughts by saying, "There's not going to be a next one. I'm not pushing another one of those out of my vagina. You're going to keep your dick away from me."

Gatz walks to her and kisses her forehead. "Anything for you, babe. I love you."

She snuggles closer to him. "I love you more."

My brother glances at me. "Thank you for coming, but this lady needs to sleep."

"I can't," Maia shrieks. "Who's going to watch her? Look at her, she's tiny. I need to protect her."

"Well, since you two are busy making decisions, we're going to go," I say, pretending to leave with Soleil.

I take only two steps before Gatz is in front of me. "You can't take my baby with you."

"What if I promise to take care of her?"

He snorts. "Uh-huh. The same way you take care of your plants?"

I glare at him. *Can he let go of that shit?*

A couple of years ago, when I moved from Vancouver to Portland, my sisters bought me a set of decent stemware, silverware, and even a few plants. Needless to say, I only have two out of three housewarming gifts. Not my fault.

Back then, I didn't know anyone locally. Who am I kidding? I still don't know many Oregonians. I'm either traveling with my hockey team to the next game, training, or coming home to be with my siblings. I couldn't tell anyone to water my plants.

"This is uncalled for. Cory and Fern shouldn't have bought me plants as a housewarming gift. I travel a lot." Sometimes I think my sisters did that on purpose so everyone could make fun of me.

Cas is so irresponsible. He can't even keep a plant alive.

Gatsby doesn't acknowledge me. He carefully takes Soleil out of my arms.

"If I'm in charge, I can take care of this little piece of sun—and keep her alive," I argue.

"Uh-huh. You're always traveling, and you don't live anywhere near San Francisco or Paradise Bay. When the season is over, you can help us take care of her."

"Really? You'll let me take care of her? Or is this another way to just give me the runaround?"

He shrugs. "We'll see."

"I can take care of her," I insist.

"Why don't you start by bringing some fries with melted cheese to her mother?"

I glance at Maia, who's finally asleep. "She has the weirdest cravings."

"It's not a craving. It's…she just likes to indulge in greasy food, and this is a good moment to pamper her."

"You want me to bring you something to eat?"

He nods. "Whatever you're having." He presses his lips into a thin line and says, "Thank you for coming."

"I wouldn't miss this."

Out of my seven siblings, Gatsby and Fern are my favorites. I know it's wrong to have preferences, but I can't help it. After Dad died and my mom went into a catatonic state, Gatz was the only one who supported me and my love of hockey. Even though his triplets—Lysander and Aslan—suggested I quit because nobody had time for my schedule.

In the beginning, he was the one who drove me anywhere I needed to be at all times. He also taught me how to drive and came to most of my games. Fern…well, that's different. She took Mom's place, and I appreciate all the sacrifices she made for us.

Whenever they need me, I'm there. Well, that's a general rule. If any of my siblings need me, I drop everything and go to them.

"Don't forget to check on Fern before heading back to Oregon."

I nod once. "Already planned for it, no worries."

As I step outside their room, I glance at Gatz's little family one last time. He got his star—Maia—and I…well, I made a mistake and missed my chance to be with who I think could've been my soul mate.

It was one of the best nights of my life and after her...well, what am I supposed to do with my life after Rys?

Chapter Ten

Rys

I'M ABOUT to fall asleep, and whose fault is that?

I should consider this... "Bad idea number... I lost count," I mumble as I close the microwave door and set up the time to reheat my leftovers.

"Are you okay?" Dan, one of my colleagues and closest friends, asks.

I nod. "Peachy." But I'm actually not.

Traveling back and forth from Portland to San Francisco is draining me. Add the occasional trip to Baker's Creek and I need a vacation—perhaps a sabbatical.

You want me managing two clinics in different states, of course I can do it. How hard can it be? I want to travel to the past and slap myself a couple of times for not only considering it, but agreeing with it. I can't keep up this pace.

Dan bobs his head a few times, takes his food from the fridge, and while setting his stuff in the other microwave, he says, "You look like you're about to wrap yourself in a blanket and quit the world. What's happening?"

"Nothing."

He nods.

"Is it because you had to travel to Baker's Creek this weekend and you won't see your hot boyfriend?" He pretends to look around and whispers, "I heard you might get fired for dating the captain of our archenemy."

I burst into laughter. What else can I do? Six months ago, when I accepted to go on a blind date with a guy who sounded too good to be true, I had no idea I was about to meet Thad Roderick, the captain of the San Jose Sharks. He's one of the best hockey players in the league—not that I follow the sport. I'm just learning about it.

Leyla Aldridge, my boss, is teaching me all she knows, which is a lot. She's not only a fan, but her brother-in-law owns the Portland Orcas. Hence, there's always someone joking that I'm going to get fired. If I wanted to date a big hockey name, they could've introduced me to an Orca player—even the captain.

Funny story, the captain of their team is Caspian Spearman, the guy I met a few years ago who said he was an actuary. Lying asshole. I knew there was something fishy about him. Thankfully it was a one-time thing and I'm over him.

Over him.

Over.

Okay, I'm still working on it. He kissed me like no one ever had done before, and sex with him was the best I've had in my entire life. Not that I've had any since him. I've been too busy.

Dan clears his throat, looking at me expectantly, so I say, "I'm sure they wouldn't fire me for that."

"So how are things with Thad the hottie?"

I shrug one shoulder. My relationship with Thad is…strange, to say the least. He's a thoughtful guy. When we go out on dates, he's amazing, but we don't see each other often. Between my schedule, his schedule, and his family always needing him, it's hard to know where I stand.

Dan raises an eyebrow. "Still no sex, huh?"

"I didn't say that."

"You don't have to, girl. What's his excuse this time? His mojo is gone if he has sex before a game? There's someone else, but has you as a backup?"

I scoff. "We're both busy." I sound irritated, which is better than fragile.

Sometimes I wonder if there's something wrong with me, but others I wonder if there's any chemistry between Thad and me. He's good looking, but I don't have the attraction I had with Caspian.

Another reason I might hate Caspian Spearman. He broke me.

Dan clears his throat. "That sounds like a total excuse from one of you. Maybe it's you, because you yearn for the one night you'll never see again."

Why does he have to bring up Cas? I'm so glad I didn't tell anyone his name or there'd be gossiping about the possibility of a love triangle. There's no such thing going on between the three of us.

I roll my eyes. "It's not an excuse."

"So this is where the gossip happens?" Leyla enters the room. "I've been wondering where my two best doctors were hiding."

"You're missing a lot, boss," Dan says. "Our girl is growing back her virginity."

I blush. He didn't just say that. "Seriously, Daniel?"

He shrugs. "It's true. When was the last time you had sex? Not since the Portland clinic opened and you moved there. What was the name of that hot mystery guy?" He snaps his fingers.

I wave a hand as if saying it doesn't matter. "It was long ago."

"But you agree this drought is weird?"

"We're waiting for the right time."

He rolls his eyes. "If my husband had told me to wait for the right time, I would've dropped his ass and searched for someone else."

Leyla laughs. "Doubtful. You love him too much." She turns her attention to me. "Are you okay? You look tired."

I nod.

"When you're ready to talk, I'm here for you, okay?" Leyla isn't just a great boss, but also a good friend.

There's nothing to say. Do I want some advice on how to take the next step with my boyfriend? I should know how to do it, but it's almost impossible to bring up sex when he's too busy and always on the run. I don't want to sound like the needy girlfriend.

What can Leyla say?

Go to his hotel room wearing nothing but a trench coat and ride that hunk? It's not a bad idea, and before I start planning a trip to Detroit so I can fuck my boyfriend, I ask, "So why did you call us to Baker's Creek, Leyla?"

"We're opening a new branch in Luna Harbor."

One thing I love about working for Leyla—other than the scholarships she gives to those who can't afford vet school—is that she wants to create more animal hospitals with her vision. She charges what's fair, she never turns away a pet, even if the owners can't afford the treatments, and she has a shelter right next door. The only thing I don't love is that she usually tries to persuade Dan or me to help her open them. Hopefully, this time she'll hire someone. I can't travel to three different places.

Dan's the one who asks, "Where's that?"

"West of Seattle," she answers.

"Another small town where you want to drop our asses? Pass," Dan says and leaves.

Leyla looks at me. "I'm not expecting to move either one of you to that branch. I want you to help me choose a candidate for that clinic."

I sigh with relief. "That sounds more like it. I don't think I can do a third commute."

She gives me a curious glance. "Are you still okay with that? We can look through the candidates and get someone to take over San Fran or Portland. Whichever place you don't want to live in."

"I…"

"Think about it. San Fran is closer to your boyfriend…" The pause she makes and the way she looks at me make me wonder what she's thinking. "Other than the sex drought, are things okay with Thad?"

"Yes."

But are they?

The lack of sex doesn't bother me as much, but…okay, it is weird that we only make out like horny teenagers, but when things get a little out of hand, he stops and disappears.

The few times I tried to bring up the subject, he diverted the conversation. Hence, I don't mention it anymore. Sometimes I wonder if that's why we double-date with his best friend, Cameron, and her husband. Is he afraid I'm going to jump him in the middle of a restaurant?

"You should talk to Hadley," Leyla mentions her sister-in-law. "She married a hockey player—and the owner of the Orcas team. Though Mills retired a year ago, she has some experience."

"Good. For a moment, I thought you were going to offer me a free subscription to the Orcas-Tinder."

She laughs and shakes her head. "Never mention that to Hadley, or she might create an app and use it to raise funds by auctioning the players via *Orcas-Tinder*."

"We could do it for the animal shelters."

"Stop it." She continues laughing. "I just think it must be tough to see the man you love only a couple of times a month."

Is it hard? It's strange, but not for the reason she thinks. I'm not in love with Thad. He checked all the boxes, but we haven't had the time to fall in love and become a real couple. We never do.

Leyla tilts her head toward the hallway. "Break time is over. Let's try to figure out what we'll do with Luna Harbor's new clinic."

"Are you building it soon?"

"Yep. We already have permits, the blueprints, and the groundbreaking ceremony is in a month. One of my brothers-in-law is involved in the project to rebuild the town. As soon as he learned we were going to open a clinic there, he and his friends took charge of the paperwork."

"If you need help, I'm here for you."

She shakes her head. "Maybe, and this is just me guessing, you need to choose one branch and stop traveling so much. The last thing I want is to lose one of my favorite doctors because she's burnt out."

"It's okay." I try my best to sound casual but I'm not sure if I accomplish much.

"I'll believe you for now, but it's okay to change your mind."

Is it?

Maybe what I need is to have a life and figure out my relationship with Thad. There are times when I feel lonely and wonder if I should at least adopt a dog or a cat from the shelter. Then, I remind myself that I'm never at home—or in the same state.

Why bother?

And for one second, I remember Cas and wonder if we'd be together if I had given him my number. He's the only guy who's made me feel...*shut up, Rys. Forget about Caspian. Focus on your life and make the best out of it.*

Chapter Eleven

Rys

WE HAVE several candidates to take over the Luna Harbor clinic. Some of them live in Seattle. I spend the rest of the day hanging at the shelter, getting acquainted with a cute black cat that could use a home, but when it's time to go to my hotel room, I decide to leave her.

I don't think I'm ready to adopt anyone, not just yet.

After I change clothes and I'm about to go to bed, I notice I have a text from Thad.

Thad: Babe, are you around?

I stare at the message for a couple of seconds before answering.

Rys: In San Fran?

Thad: Yep.

Rys: No. I told you I had to come to Baker's Creek and I'm staying in town for a week.

Thad: I thought we could do something this week.

Rys: Rain check?

Thad: Of course. Can you come to Vegas for the All-Star Game?

It's hard to keep up with his schedule, and instead of checking the spreadsheet on my phone, I text him back.

Rys: Is that the one you asked me to change your reservation so it's under my name?

Thad: Yep, that one.

I check the calendar. That's in February—in just a couple of weeks. Do I want to go? What's the point? I'd have to talk to Leyla about it. Since I don't want to disappoint him, I answer what my father usually tells us when he's not sure about something.

Rys: I don't know... I can see if my boss can give me the weekend off.

Thad: You work too much. Come out and play with me, Rys.

Rys: I'll try to make it happen.

Thad: I miss you.

Okay, this conversation is going from strange to *you're entering the twilight zone.* I can hear the theme song of the show playing in the back of my mind.

Rys: Is everything okay?

Thad: Can a guy miss his girlfriend?

Rys: Of course you can. It's just...nice to hear it.

Thad: Do you miss me?

Again with the weirdness. Do I miss him? The answer should

be of course I do, but how can I when we barely see each other. This relationship isn't working and maybe I should try harder. It seems as if he's trying, isn't he?

Rys: I do.

Okay, that's a white lie. Maybe with time I'll learn to miss him, even love him.

Thad: Why don't you fly to me? I'll pay for the ticket.

Rys: I would, but it's actually too late to catch a plane. You should visit your family.

Thad: They're busy today. If you were around, I could teach you to have a little fun with Thad.

Rys: Next time I'm in town.

Thad: Or Vegas. Let's meet in Vegas, babe.

That's seven weeks from today. Isn't that a little too long? If we're going to try to make this work, maybe we should start sooner.

Rys: I could try to sneak out tomorrow. Unless you plan on playing golf with Roger?

Thad: There's no Roger. He and Cameron went on some stupid trip this weekend.

Rys: Everything okay?

Thad: Yeah, Cam and I had a fight.

Rys: She's your best friend. I'm sure you'll make up soon.

Thad: I…let's not talk about her.

Rys: You guys are like brother and sister. It'll be fine.

Thad: Come with me to Vegas.

Rys: I won't make any promises, but I'll try to be there. After all, the reservation is under my name. I might surprise you.

Thad: How about a preview?

Rys: I could…but maybe I'll make you wait.

Thad: I'm so glad I have you, Rys. I promise things will be different.

Rys: Okay.

I don't know what that promise entails, but if he plans on making things work, I can do just the same.

How hard can it be?

Actually, what changed? Is it weird that it's happening just as he had a fight with Cam and Roger?

Chapter Twelve

Rys

NEVER IN MY life have I been to Vegas. Ever. The immediate immersion into wheels of color and slot machines takes me by surprise as I walk through the airport, but it does add a certain ambiance.

My blood is already thrumming with excitement when I climb into an Uber and give the driver the name of the hotel where I know my boyfriend is staying.

This has been seven weeks in the making. Things are going to change tonight. Well, they've been changing daily. We've been texting daily about everything and nothing. It's as if everything changed over the past seven weeks and he's now committed to our relationship.

When I left Portland, I hinted to Leyla that we might need someone for one of the clinics. I didn't tell her that I'm probably choosing San Francisco.

I want to be a thousand percent sure Thad and I aren't only compatible, but ready to take the next step. I don't mean living together, just having a real relationship. Texting him for seven weeks isn't the same as seeing him almost daily, sharing meals, and finding time to really hang out.

If it wasn't for the holidays and his hectic traveling schedule, we could've seen each other a few times. He doesn't know today we'll be seeing each other, it's a surprise.

Suddenly, I almost break into a sweat. What if it all goes wrong this weekend?

All day I've had this gut-wrenching feeling. I checked on my parents twice to make sure neither one of them fell down the stairs and was bleeding from a broken neck. Milly, my sister, is also doing fine. Is it me?

I let go of the death grip on my weekender bag as I try to calm myself. Nothing bad is going to happen. I've had sex before. Thad is safe and…well, now I'm concerned if he'll be okay with me.

Though he invited me several times to spend the weekend with him, I couldn't promise that I would. In fact, I was supposed to be here yesterday. Last weekend when I couldn't confirm, Thad was disappointed, but not upset, that I couldn't make it.

"He's going to be happy when he sees you," I mutter under my breath.

"Is everything okay?" the Uber driver—Raquel—asks.

"Yes. This is spectacular. I've seen the Vegas strip in movies, but in person—"

"It's amazing, isn't it?"

"You must love living here."

"It's entertaining. I can have as many jobs as I want. Uber driver, grocery delivery, waitress—there's never a dull moment." She smiles as she stops in front of the hotel. "Have fun!"

I stare at the luminous building and take a deep breath.

What if Thad has other plans?

This might've been a bad idea. I force out a harsh, cleansing breath. I'm just being insecure, and that's not who I am. Fortunately, it's late enough in the day that I'm pretty sure he'll be back at the hotel for a short window of time before going out again with some of his buddies from the other teams. He'd sent me a text about an hour ago before he headed into an interview. I open the chat to check the time.

Rys: *Where are you? Back at the hotel or already out having fun?*

He doesn't respond. Maybe he's busy, or taking a shower, or…the endless possibilities. I plan on going to his room and surprising him. If he's not there, I'll put on the lingerie I bought for the weekend and wait for him—in bed.

Since I made the reservation for Thad, I have the electronic key in my app. I should stop by the reception and make sure he switched my credit card for his. We might be trying to have a more serious relationship, but I'm not ready to spend six hundred dollars a night because he likes his privacy.

I'm practically bouncing toward the elevator. Everything has gone perfectly to plan. Thad is going to be ecstatic to see me. He'd been really disappointed when I couldn't come. By the time I get to the eighth floor, I'm antsy and excited.

His room is a long walk from the elevator, and I can't help but grin stupidly the whole time. I get to his door and regret not changing into the very short, sparkly dress I bought last week. Oh well, jeans and a t-shirt will have to do. I check my makeup on my phone camera and nod to myself in satisfaction. Since this night is going to be epic, I decide to film my entrance so I can record his face.

I scan the electronic card into the handle and slowly push

open the door. I'm prepared for him to be in the shower or maybe sitting around, but instead, I hear the frantic sound of flesh slapping against flesh and moaning.

Okay, he's watching porn. This is like the episode in *Friends* when Monica catches Chandler watching…well, he changed the channel to a shark documentary. How is Thad going to react when he's caught? I don't mind. We can have sex while it's on, it might be hotter.

Is it?

I know some people who have sex while watching porn. No judgment here. To each their own. If this is how Thad likes it, I'm okay.

At least, that's what I think until I see him. Thad is in his bed alright, but instead of watching porn, he's fucking another woman. It takes several seconds for my brain to process what I'm seeing.

It's at that moment when the woman he's with notices me and gives out a yelp of surprise. She slaps Thad on the arm as he continues to thrust and grunt. "Babe, I fucking miss you so much. Don't leave me again, it's okay if you want to stay with Roger."

The words feel like slaps. I watch in absolute, gaping horror as he very clearly comes inside her. I want to run, but I can't actually peel my eyes away.

"Cameron," I hear myself say to the woman who is staring back at me, equally horrified. "I had no idea you were coming this weekend. He mentioned you two fought, and obviously, you forgot to bring Roger along."

I'm impressed by how steady I sound as Thad finally realizes something's wrong. He twists his torso around, his dick hanging limp, and he's not even wearing a condom.

"Rys?" he asks dumbly, frowning. "Why is your phone directed at us?"

I cringe when I realize I caught the last few minutes of their fucking on video. There goes my great moment filmed for our future. "So, I guess things between you and Cam are okay? Is

Roger...you know, okay with this arrangement? I'm just wondering since you seem to be spending so much time together."

"You can't say a word," Cameron says at the same time Thad mumbles, "It's not what you think."

"I think you're fucking your best friend." I focus on Cameron. "And you're cheating on your husband. And you both made a complete idiot out of me."

"That's exactly why I got you to date him. So you could cover for us. Do you really think he would go out with someone like *you*?"

"If you're saying that to hurt my feelings so I'll leave here sobbing...well, I just simply can't take you seriously when you're naked with *my* boyfriend. Lashing out at me won't take away what's happening right now. You're a cheater."

She sneers and glares at Thad. "Are you going to let her insult me?"

Thad's staring at me. There's a certain regret in his eyes. It's as if he knows he's screwed up his chances with me but doesn't want to lose whatever he has with her.

For a second, I feel bad because maybe he's been in love with Cam for a long time but will never be the man of her life. But it's just pity and nothing more. I can't help but say, "Something tells me this has been going on for years. Just remember you'll only be the fun, hot guy she fucks—never the one she loves."

"Shut up," she says.

I scoff. "So, you don't deny that I'm right?"

I give him a look of pity. "I'll just leave you to it, then." I nod to myself like I'm some kind of broken bobblehead. Thad gapes at me like there's something he has to say but he just can't form the words. I take a deep breath and steady myself. "Enjoy, and whatever's between us is over—not that it ever started."

I spin on my heel and speed walk out of the room. I want to slam the door behind me, but because my life is apparently a dramedy of errors, the door refuses to slam and instead gently drifts closed behind me.

Thad doesn't follow me or even call after me. I manage to wait until the elevator doors close, leaving me alone in the small box before I let the wave of emotion crash into me. It takes me out at the knees, and I have to grab the brass bar for balance as I sway forward. I'm not crying—I absolutely refuse to cry—but I can feel how badly I'm shaking.

I'm so fucking angry I want to smash something. Maybe go to a kickboxing class. It's a blur from the elevator to the bar, but I somehow find myself on a barstool. I must look as shaken as I feel because the bartender looks concerned.

"You already have a few?" he asks, but it's not unkind. "Maybe I can just get you a seltzer?"

It takes a few tries to string words together.

"Not drunk," I say finally, which probably isn't that convincing. "Just having a..."

How do I finish the sentence?

Bad night, day, weekend...is it even bad? I'm shaking with rage but it's never bad to find out that the guy you wanted to be the love of your life is just a scumbag. I liked him just fine and we could've been something if either one of us had tried.

He fucking used me.

Okay, that's what has my blood boiling.

After a long sigh, I say, "I found my boyfriend with his lover. Apparently, they were more than *just friends,* and I was just the cover-up so they could fuck whenever they wanted."

He flinches. "Ouch."

I sit on a barstool, regulating my breathing with every yoga trick I've ever learned. I must pass the sobriety test because he finally throws his towel over his shoulder and nods at me. "Alright, anything in particular I can get you, then?"

"Vodka, tequila, scotch...your strongest liquor," I say. "Maybe some soda too, but the latter is totally optional."

He snorts at me but has a perfectly poured vodka soda in front of me in less than a minute. I take a grateful gulp and immediately feel a little steadier.

That is, until someone clears their throat next to me and leans against the bar to my right. For a moment, I freeze, completely not ready to face Thad or Cameron yet, but when I look up, it's worse, much worse.

Caspian Spearman stands right in front of me.

Okay, so this night *can* get worse.

Chapter Thirteen

Caspian

I<small>T'S</small> A<small>LL-STAR</small> weekend in Vegas, which means a lot of media and a lot of gritting my teeth through pretending to like some of the biggest assholes in the league. Not to mention the ridiculous stunts they make us try to pull off like we're not all tired and probably nursing secret injuries already.

Last year, I'd gotten out of the whole weekend because the

team had sent our new, hot young rookie, but this year the vote had landed on me again.

Lucky, lucky me. I'd much rather be taking the long weekend to spend with my family like the rest of my team, but instead, I'm answering the same questions over and over.

I like my job for the most part—not much to complain about when you play a game for a living—but the media is the worst part and things like this are all about the media. I don't understand why they want to know about my personal life—most of the other guys don't get it as bad, but it seems like they're always probing me for some mention of a girlfriend or my family when I just want to talk about the game and leave.

It's gotten worse lately, or maybe it just feels that way since my mother has been extremely interested in my lack of a love life. With eight children, everyone would think she's too busy to focus just on me.

Technically, Helicopter Dawn can multitask, but her focus on my love life—or lack of it—might lie in the fact that I'm next in line. Luckily, I live hundreds of miles away from her. She can only nag me via text or when I visit home. I avoid Paradise Bay like the plague.

Once the mock games are over and prizes are given out, I'm allowed to slip through the back doors and into the basement, where I gratefully get into the rental car. If I could have, I would've flown back to Portland tonight, but it's too much to get on a plane after this circus without at least getting some sleep. I head back to the hotel instead. Most of the players stay there when we're in town, so no doubt I'll see a few of them back there as well.

Players at All-Star weekend tend to group into the old guys with families and the young guys who just want to get trashed and party. By all rights, I should be in the latter camp since I'm single, but the idea of a night out in Vegas after a full day of playing sounds like a nightmare. I'd done plenty of that in my rookie year and beyond.

The same bartender from the night before greets me at the

bar and slides me a single malt on the rocks just as quickly. I give him a nod in thanks and slide a bill across to him before taking the drink and retreating into one of the darker corners—less chance of being spotted that way.

The bar is supposed to be for hotel guests only, but that's never stopped an enterprising fan or puck bunny before. Besides, earlier I was positive I'd seen Thad Roderick, lord of the assholes and captain of the San Jose Sharks, lurking around, and I'd rather go back for another round of interviews than pretend to enjoy having a drink with him. Total douche.

Thinking of Thad Roderick pricks me with the memory of *her* on his arm the last time my team had been in San Jose. I take a big gulp of whiskey and savor the burn. I thought I'd been hallucinating when I saw *her*. Her being Rys, the woman I'd spent the most unbelievable night of my life with. But when she turned and looked at me, her expression suddenly changed into anger.

As if I did something to her. I recall having a great time with her. No promises or expectations. Do I regret that? Yes, every second, because from the first kiss I wanted to get to know her, and yet, I let her go.

I'd left quickly after that—no need to torture myself with seeing her with that huge dick. It's not like I ever had a real shot with her, did I? Long-distance relationships never work, and women are… But I can't just lump her with the rest.

Sure, she's dating the douchiest guy in America, but I know she's smart, funny, and sensible.

Why is she dating that guy?

Well, I'm not sure if they're still together. The woman I saw him with earlier is so much different than Rys. Did he break up with her?

The biggest question is, why am I thinking of her?

I take my phone out of my pocket and thumb it open for something to distract me. There are a couple of texts from Gatsby with new pictures of Soleil. She's officially eight weeks old. I wonder if Fern will be sending us updates of the twins when they're born.

There are several texts on the Orcas team chat of the guys chirping me for different parts of the broadcast. Stephens, the absolute asshole, has forgone teasing for just posting a picture of himself shirtless on the beach with a fucking coconut. I send him a middle-finger emoji and lock the phone.

I turn to one of the big TVs playing a baseball game and settle in with what's left of my drink. The bar is quiet except for the soft hum of classical music, and the lights are low enough that the TVs have a kind of halo around them where they're strung up high above the bar. It's a surprisingly quiet spot for a Vegas bar, and I'm happy to spend another hour or two unwinding here in peace.

Except something makes me turn toward the entrance. That's when I see her. Rys looking just as beautiful as always, though her face is tense.

I frown, wondering what happened to her.

Stay away from her, Spearman!

But what if she needs me?

Chapter Fourteen

Caspian

RYS APPEARS at the bar as if conjured by the mere passing thought of her. Once my brain gets past the immediate glitch on how insanely hot she looks—long, curled hair loose around her shoulders and curves wrapped in a pair of jeans—I realize she looks upset.

Not like she's been crying, but definitely some flavor of upset.

I watch her from my seat, waiting to see if the douche will appear to rescue her. Maybe she's with friends or another guy. This answers my question from earlier. They both moved on and are onto the next person.

How can she do it?

No, really, how can she move on from something so significant?

I'm obviously projecting here.

My eyes shift back to the entrance of the bar that opens into the lobby. I'm waiting for Roderick to appear, but after she sits, the bartender serves her, and she downs what looks like a vodka soda. It's pretty apparent Rys isn't waiting for anyone.

I play with my empty glass, the ice cubes tinkling their way around the bottom as I think about how to handle the situation. I could ignore her and bank on her not seeing me back here. What if she's upset though? Where is Roderick? Was he the one who made her look this way? I continue watching for another minute before I sigh at my empty glass. I know it's inevitable that I'll get up and talk to her. There's no way I would ever pass up the chance to talk to her again.

She doesn't see me coming, and I slide up to the barstool right next to her, under the raised eyebrow of the bartender. I nod at him and push my empty glass across the counter for a refill before I clear my throat to get Rys's attention. She freezes, but when she turns to me and realizes who it is next to her, all I see is unfiltered despair.

"Gotta say, not the usual response I get at the bar," I joke, although my heart isn't really in it. I had thought she looked stunning from far away. Up close, she's devastatingly gorgeous. I can't help but flash back to her naked in bed.

Her lips purse unhappily, but then she takes another swig of her drink and shakes out her shoulders.

"Cas," she acknowledges me.

"You look upset," I say. "Roderick do something to you?"

She gives me a sharp look. Her mouth twists in disgust, but she doesn't immediately respond, like she's considering the question. I am not prepared in any way for her dry, deadpan answer.

"I just saw him fucking his best friend in the hotel room I booked for him"—she lets out a shaky angry breath—"for us."

The bartender, right on cue, brings me a fresh whiskey, and I have never been more thankful to have a drink in my hand. I am absolutely speechless.

What a fucking asshole!

But I'm not surprised, this is his MO.

"He invited me out here. It's not like I decided to come out because I'm clingy or needy," she continues. "But I wasn't sure if I could make it. Work has been hectic, and I...anyway, things changed, and I decided to surprise him." She laughs bitterly.

The laughter goes on and on. I get the feeling I'm not strictly necessary for this conversation, but I'm here until she forces me to leave, so I listen. She swirls her drink around in her glass, looking absolutely forlorn. "They fucking used me. I thought he was safe, but the joke's on me."

"Nothing funny here," I say. It seems to remind her that I'm here at all.

Her eyes narrow as she looks at me and frowns.

"Caspian Spearman," she enunciates very carefully. "You are not an actuary."

It surprises a laugh out of me, and I shake my head. "No," I agree. "I'm not."

"Why lie?" she asks, reading my mind. "I knew there was something wrong with you. Like Cameron said—"

She suddenly stops and presses her lips together. Okay, so maybe I've got a clue as to why she's upset at me. I recall she hates liars, and in her book, I lied when we met. It wasn't like that.

I sigh.

I point toward her empty glass, and she nods, so I ask the bartender to pour her another.

"If you recall, you're the one who came up with that obscure career. I chose not to correct you," I say honestly. "Sometimes it's nice just to be…normal. You made me feel like I mattered as a person and not as Cas the hockey player or one of the Spearman siblings. I made several mistakes that night, but it's still one of my favorites—if not my favorite memory."

She does that cute thing of fidgeting with her bottom lip while humming in thought. Her eyes flick back to the darker corners of the bar. I take the cue and nod in the direction of the table I had been sitting at. We both slide into the dark leather booth, safely ensconced in shadows. The moment is awkward as we face each other fully for the first time.

"So, bad night, huh?" I ask, leaning into the awkwardness.

She smiles wryly at me and takes a drink.

"You seeing anyone?" she asks.

"Nah." I'm not about to remind her that I don't date.

Should I even mention I haven't been with anyone since we hooked up?

I've never quite been able to get her out of my mind when looking at other women. I look at her now and know that I'm totally screwed.

But she moved on. She forgot you.

"I'm officially done with the dating scene," she says grimly.

That's code for *men suck, and each one I've dated is a scumbag.* At least, that's what it'd mean to Cory, my youngest sister.

"So, you've had a lot of game?"

"No. I've been too busy at the animal hospital to go out. The blind date with Thad was my first. We seemed to be compatible. The second time I saw him, it was a double date with…"

She burst into laughter. A maniacal crazy laughter she can't contain. "I get it now."

I furrow my eyebrows. "What are we talking about?"

"During our second date, he introduced me to Cameron—his best friend—and her husband. It was a double date. It made me feel welcome, but now I believe she was there for a different reason. Cam was there to approve of me. I was their perfect alibi."

"You lost me."

"If Thad had a girlfriend, her husband would never suspect that they were lovers... And fuck in the hotel rooms. All those times I booked his room under my name, it was so everyone would think *I* was the one with him. A few weeks ago, when they fought...he wanted to try to make this relationship work. That's what changed. We were supposed to have sex this weekend—for the first time—because they weren't together anymore."

It takes me a few seconds to catch up with her relationship with Thad. "You're broken-hearted but you never had sex with him?"

That doesn't sound like him. He'd be fucking both, why would he be loyal to a woman who's married?

"Are you following me? I never got to fall in love with him. I'm not sad but angry. So fucking mad. He used me. They used me. That's it. I'm done."

"Done?"

"Dating is not for me," she answers.

"Or you're just dating assholes," I point out without telling her she was dating the biggest asshole in the league.

"Not anymore," she says.

She's pouting at her newly empty glass, and it's adorable. "I told him it was over—but it never began."

"So, you're here. In Vegas. Newly single." I suppress the smile.

"Technically, I was never in a relationship. What a joke! It's not like I planned my life around him, but I was trying to..."

I lean my elbows on the table. "What were you trying?"

"My little sister has two children. She finally married her longtime fiancé. Though Mom hates men, she's on my case because I'm single. What am I waiting for, Prince Harry?" She leans forward and gives me a severe look. "I shouldn't. He's happily married. I should just jump on whatever looks decent. Look at Milly. She found someone. Why can't I?"

I can't help but laugh at what I think might be the imitation of her mother.

"So, you're being pressured and thought—"

"No. I was going to give the guy and the relationship a real chance. I confess that in the past few months, I was okay with the whole 'we're platonic' thing because we both travel a lot."

"You live in San Jose?"

"No. I have an apartment in Portland but travel every other week to San Francisco—that's where we met."

I take a swig of my drink and finish it. This calls for more than a drink. "I was going to offer to get you another vodka, but I have a better idea."

"You better not be about to say 'let's go up to my room,' or I swear I'll…" She sighs. "Listen, you're hot, and sex with you is great, but—"

"Ouch, way to put a guy down."

"It's just…why bother? We know you're a player. How many women do you have as your booty calls?"

I laugh, full-chested and loud enough to attract a few looks from other patrons.

"None. You really don't believe that I don't date or sleep around, do you?"

She shakes her head. "You lied to me."

"By omission."

"It's all the same."

I know it was a mistake not to tell her who I was or ask her for her number, but I can't apologize for all the stupid things I did in the past. Fuck, she lives in Portland. We could've made it work.

Not the point, Spearman.

"So, we should go out on the casino floor and throw away some money. I'll pony up for you so you can feed machines as long as you want."

"A dangerous proposition, Mr. Spearman," she says, but the way she's smiling tells me she's going to say yes. "What if I'm some high roller?"

"I'd love to see it."

Chapter Fifteen

Rys

WHO KNEW the slot machines would, in fact, make me feel better?

In the beginning, it was a mindless game of pushing and hoping for the best. Until it wasn't just that. I was making some money. I'm not talking thousands, but my very first pull nets me fifty dollars. So...I chase the high for another hour until the casino card is empty.

"I think this is over," I say.

Cas shakes his head. "We have all night."

And so he puts an ungodly amount of money on the casino card. Under normal circumstances, I would feel bad about throwing away his money on shitty Hulk-themed slot machines, but Cas keeps my drink topped up and plays right alongside me, so it instead feels like something we're getting away with.

"Oh, I like that one." I point to the Wheel of Fortune corner and pull at Cas's arm until he peels away from the machine he's at and follows me. I pat his bicep like he's a good sport about this. I forgot how amazing it was to be with him. It's like having your best friend around, even when I barely know him.

He slings an arm around my shoulders. He smells like wood, tobacco, and him. I still remember that scent. It's like it never left me. But it did, and after all these years, I know better. Though, I definitely can't fault me for falling into his bed.

"We should get something to eat after this round," he says. "Balance out all that liquor with some guac and chips. Probably fries."

"No. We're having fun."

"Rys?"

I exhale, letting my lips flutter. He's definitely right, now that I think about it. My stomach even rumbles right on cue. I press a hand to it and laugh.

"I love guac—maybe some nachos with lots of sour cream, cheese, and jalapeños."

He offers me his arm again, and I thread mine through his. It's easy—being with Cas. Kind of scary easy.

Less than ten minutes later, I'm happily stuffing my face with what might be the best guacamole in Vegas, when two women approach our table. I look up at them in surprise, but it's not me they're looking at. In fact, I might as well not be there at all.

"Sorry to bother you," one of them says to Cas, not sounding sorry at all. "But you're Cassie, right?"

Cas has already transitioned into a fully robotized version of himself, complete with a plastic smile. He probably looks exactly the same to strangers, but to my eyes, he's stiff and uncomfortable as the women crowd closer to him and beg for a picture. He stands and puts his arms around them. One of the women hands me her phone to snap the picture without so much as a please.

At least they leave pretty quickly when it's clear Cas isn't interested in carrying on any kind of conversation with them. When they're gone, he relaxes a little, but not fully. The carefree mood has spoiled a little.

"Sorry," Cas says, smoothing his rumpled button-down. "Was kinda hoping we could avoid all that."

I shrug. I'm pretty used to the treatment by now—I'd been dating Thad for several months, and it was pretty par for the course to be ignored or outright sneered at by fans like I'm just a piece of decoration. It's not like I have a whole-ass doctorate and my career and all that.

Honestly, I don't know how the WAGs handle this for so many years. I get the impression we're all just inconvenient details for the fans, no matter what we do when we're not with the player we're dating.

"Used to it," I say. I dunk my chip in the guac and eat it slowly. "Maybe if you went full Clark Kent, you could pull it off."

"Pull what off?"

"The whole actuary thing."

He laughs, and his eyes crinkle at the corners. His skin is tan, even though I know he's based out of Portland most of the year —maybe he continues helping his brother in the vineyard. Is that what makes him so tan and hot?

I forcibly pull my eyes away from him and back to my bowl of tortilla chips, taking the last one. Would it be weird to order more? I scrutinize my plate carefully and don't even notice when Cas waves the waitress over.

"I think we'll need a large order of fries, a refill on the basket of chips, and some chicken tenders, please," he says, and I look up in surprise. He grins at me. "You looked way too sad about your last chip over there."

"I didn't know you were psychic too," I gasp playfully.

The waitress looks at us both tiredly and just flips her book closed before walking off toward the kitchen. I stifle my snort of laughter as she leaves.

"You would think she was tired of dealing with a bunch of drunks or something," Cas whispers across the table.

"I'm not drunk," I insist. "You are."

This is a blatant falsehood. He nursed the same beer for over an hour as I ran my way through at least a bottle of Merlot, three different kinds of cocktails, and a shot of tequila. Clearly, he's happy to babysit me on the worst night of my life.

"You know," I say as I think that. "This isn't the worst night."

"Wow," he says drily. "High praise."

I let my chin drop into my hand and smile sarcastically at him before grabbing up the last few fries on his plate.

"You know what I mean," I say. "Without you, this night would have been shitty."

"It doesn't necessarily need to be over." It's the first time all night that he's openly suggested something other than drinking and playing around on the casino floor.

I lift my eyebrows at him before dropping my eyes back to my water. I shake my head.

"I don't think I'm quite up for rebound sex yet," I say, trying to lighten the suddenly heavy air.

"Wow, I meant we could go fly around the Grand Canyon or see some late-night show. I heard the Backstreet Boys want you back." He grins.

I chuckle. "That's a good one."

He sits back in the booth with comically wide eyes that try to communicate his absolute innocence. "Or we can do what you said...sex."

"Ummm, that's not what I want."

"Okay, I have a better plan. Do you trust me?"

No, but what do I have to lose?

Chapter Sixteen

Caspian

I STILL DON'T UNDERSTAND how, but she fits.

That's been true since the first time we met. Rys and I just mold into each other without even trying. She's like an old friend who I haven't spoken to in years. Rys is a rainy evening next to the fireplace. The sound of my skates sliding through the ice—accelerating, calming, exciting. All the emotions that bring me joy.

Do I want to have sex with her? Badly.

Not that I would act on the urge.

Not today.

I plan on doing the one thing I thought wouldn't be possible a few years ago. Fall in love with her. It's not going to happen overnight. As my father used to say, Rome wasn't built overnight—or was it in one day? I can't remember, but that doesn't matter. This time I'm ready to make things happen between us.

It'll be easy, as many things are with Rys. She lives in Portland, and so do I. I'll find a way to meet with her. If she's in San Francisco...

I have an apartment there too. It used to belong to Gatsby. It's located in one of Aslan's properties. The moment Gatz moved in with Maia, I called dibs on it.

Having a place in San Francisco allows me to visit my family without couch surfing in my siblings' homes. Love the sibs, but I'd much rather have a nine-hour break from them. Not that I get that much. Heath lives in the penthouse—above my place—and Lysander lives on the same floor I do.

I should ask Rys where she lives when she's in San Francisco. Maybe I can plan my schedule around hers. We could see each other in both cities.

"This is too easy," she says, interrupting my plans.

"Pressing buttons and matching the image?"

"Yeah, I want a challenge."

"Blackjack?"

"No. I'm not a fan of the number twenty-one," she says with a straight face.

"What does that have to do with playing blackjack?" There has to be some obscure reason behind it.

"My twenty-first birthday was the worst of my life. The twenty-first of every month is usually a clusterfuck. Mom got married on the twenty-first of December, and that day she calls to remind me how awful my father was. See, I'll lose."

"How about roulette?"

"Yes, let's try that one. What's the strategy on that one? I need to know all the moves." She bursts into an adorable laughter.

"Have you ever been to Vegas?"

"Nope."

Okay, that explains so much, including why she looks like a kid in a candy store.

"It's about luck." I explain to her the different bets she can make.

"There's no strategy. It's pretty much like the lottery. You set your chips on the number, numbers, or colors you want and wait to see where the marble falls into. There's no science, but it keeps people entertained and losing money *all* night long."

"Okay, I think I can do it. But we can practice by watching first. Then I can see if I'm good at guessing."

Since this is her night, I agree with it.

"I bet you it's going to fall into a black number," she whispers.

"The bets are supposed to go on the table."

She smirks. "I'm practicing."

"Okay, that's fair. What do you want to bet?"

"If I win..." She narrows her gaze. "You buy me another one of those martinis with fruit."

"Strawberry or peach?"

"Surprise me." Maybe I should surprise her with water because she's a little tipsy.

Since this is a two-person game, I ask, "What do I get if I win?"

"What do you want?"

I stare at her lips. A kiss? No, I'm not kissing her while she's carrying this buzz. We can discuss us tomorrow, or maybe after I know that things between her and Roderick are over. She might swear that she's only angry, but I'm sure that after a six-month relationship, she has to be heartbroken. Doesn't she?

"There has to be something you want," she insists. "If not, you can think about a dare."

"So, if it's red, I can dare you to do something?"

She's watching the roulette. "Uh-huh, now be quiet."

And, of course, she wins. I bring her a strawberry martini and get myself a scotch. We watch three more games before she says, "I'm ready."

"To play?"

"No. Another dare. If it lands on red seven, I win. What's your number?"

We should find something else to do, but instead of saying that, I humor her. "Red twenty-seven."

"Is that your lucky number?"

"Why would you ask?"

"It's your jersey number," she mumbles.

I can't help but smirk when I say, "You know?"

"Obviously. I watched you play a couple of times."

"You did?"

"When you played the Sharks," she answers, and my hopes fly out the window.

"Oh, while visiting *the boyfriend*," I mumble, almost angry.

"Let's not go there." She finishes her martini and focuses on the roulette.

"Black twenty-one," the dealer shouts.

Her shoulders slump. "See, I told you the number twenty-one hates me."

"That's ridiculous."

"I lost to black twenty-one. What other proof do you need?"

She decides to stop playing roulette. Not that we placed a bet on the table. However, we continue to dare each other. It goes from her flirting with the guy at the bar to me asking some random guy on the strip to sign my chest.

"But you're Cassie. Caspian Spearman. The captain of the Orcas." The guy stares at me, then at my pec. "And you want my autograph?"

"Yep." I sound casual. This doesn't affect me at all.

Okay, maybe I should've drunk a few beers before agreeing to this. I hope she doesn't digress and suggest something like going to watch the Magic Kings. With my luck, that piece of information might get to my family. Elliot, my brother-in-law, owns the strip-club franchise. They'll want to know all about the girl who dragged me to watch the show. We Spearmans are supportive—we're also highly nosy.

The guy in front of me stares at the pen and then looks around. "Where's the camera?"

"That's a good idea. Take a selfie, too," Rys says.

We do as she says. She takes the camera and goes to my social media. "What's your handle? And what do you do for a living?" she asks the guy.

Suddenly she says, "Hanging out with my favorite dentist. Keep it tooth."

The guy frowns and keeps walking after that.

"You posted that on social media?"

Her eyes crinkle with satisfaction. "You lost, remember?"

"I bet you wouldn't post anything on your social media," I dare her.

"Pssshhh… I would…if I had any."

"Well then, let's open you an account." I grab her phone and set it up, picking the handle @puppyluv4lifeRys. "Let's see what we can post of you."

"I can audition for a strip club," she suggests.

She could, but I want that to be *just* for me. "Nope. That's too easy, and there might not be auditions at this time."

"We can go and witness some weddings at the chapel. Be witnessesses of their love." She slurs too many s's and that's a sign that maybe we should call it a night.

"You're drunk."

"No, still buzzing, but I'm aware of what's happening."

"So whose love are we witnessing?"

"The people who marry, and you can pay for their licenses. It'll be your good deed of the day."

"Okay. I can do that. Let me call an Uber. Let's go to the chapel."

Chapter Seventeen

Rys

THE FIRST THING I notice when I fuzzily come out of the sleep fugue I'd been in is that something is pinching my finger. I pull my hand out from underneath the pillow, hoping that will solve the problem so I can go back to sleep, but whatever it is remains firmly on my hand. I blink in the dim light of the hotel room at what appears to be a very, *very* large diamond and a matching gold band.

So large it must be fake. It's probably some piece from a gumball machine.

I bring it closer to my face and look at it for a long minute before a flash of last night comes back.

I sit up with a gasp. That's when I notice I'm only wearing a pair of men's boxer briefs, and I'm not in my room.

With mounting horror, I look over to my left to see a man's broad shoulders. My mind is rapidly moving through disaster scenarios as I realize, at the very least, this man's skin is far too tan to be Thad, so at least I hadn't ended up back in bed with that absolute asshole. Not that I saw him after last night's fiasco...*did I see him*?

I groan. "Why can't I remember much of what happened?"

I try harder, and finally, my mind begins to catch up with the events of after I landed in Vegas.

The man now known as Cheating Asshole and I broke up after I caught him in bed with his best friend. The reminder of what she said makes me fume. I'm back to seeing red and wanting to punch someone—preferably him. And then there was... Caspian Spearman.

I met Cas.

Cas, the guy who lied to me when we met. The one I had trouble forgetting, the one that...what did we do after?

"Arrrgh..." I can't remember.

Last night remains a blur of drinks and bright colors in my mind. I'm so incredibly hungover that every new memory of the night before makes my head hurt even worse. Just for peace of mind, I peek over the shoulders of my bedmate and confirm it is Cas.

It's a relief to see that at least I can remember that much. This must be his hotel room...a very luxurious room.

The blackout curtains are drawn, only letting in a small sliver of light into the cavernous room. I think I can make out the shape of some rumpled clothes on the floor. *My clothes*?

How did I end up wearing *just* Cas's underpants?

I can't believe I had sex with him—and I can't remember doing it at all. There's no smell of sex or a feel that we… I stare back at my finger.

We're not married, are we?

Panic chokes me. Cas is sleeping, or at least doing a very convincing job of pretending to. My eyes adjust to the dim light enough to see delicate black lines across his back that slowly start to re-arrange themselves into something familiar. I look at the inside of my arm. The drawings are almost exactly the same. It's a constellation. Not just any constellation, either. My constellation.

Polaris is so lightly outlined on his skin that it almost looks like someone had taken a pen and drawn on him. I can't help but lick the tip of my finger and gently rub at his skin.

Was I so drunk that I drew on him? But the ink doesn't budge, and I can feel the slightly raised texture of a tattoo. I peer at it more closely. Surely he didn't do this last night too?

Rubbing at the ink also brings the ridiculous chunky diamond on my finger back into focus. I look at it in absolute bafflement.

"The fuck did we do?" I mutter. I definitely don't know enough about diamonds to know if it's real, but considering who I'm in bed with, it's probably more likely that it is. "Fuck."

I couldn't think of a single word that wasn't a swear at the moment.

"What's wrong?" Cas asks sleepily, and the sound of his voice makes me jump. I swat at his shoulder.

"Why don't you look for yourself?" I ask irritably.

He turns over to me in bed and squints. I pointedly hold up the sheet to shield my still bare breasts even though it's more out of reflex than genuine modesty.

"I don't see anything immediately alarming," he says after a moment. His hand snakes under the sheets to brush against my ass, and I shiver. I scoot myself out of reach, and he makes a sad sound as his hand reaches for me.

"Why do I have a ring on my finger?" I ask, tired of waiting for him to catch up.

"You don't remember?" he asks, and he sounds way too amused for the situation at hand, in my opinion.

"Cas." I can't keep the rising panic out of my voice.

He snorts and props himself up on a pillow. It's entirely unfair how beautiful he looks. Not hungover at all while I feel like a train wreck.

"We were at the chapel, and after watching six couples get married, you wanted to do it too."

"And you let me?"

"Yeah, you needed to have fun. I couldn't say no. I made sure to call my agent's assistant so they wouldn't file it in the state. It's harmless—and a dare."

"How can that be?"

"The state of Nevada doesn't just let anyone get married. Usually, you need to file the marriage license the next day or within the first week—I can't remember what they explained at the chapel, but I swear this isn't binding. We were just fooling around. You seriously don't remember?"

I rub my temples and try very hard to piece together some of the vibrant puzzle pieces of last night. I did remember meeting up with a few other players in the middle of our game of dares, sometime between a high-stakes round of poker and having a guy sign Cas's ass. I remember going to a chapel and laughing. A lot of laughing. I look down at the ring and then hold it out to him in silent inquiry.

He kisses my hand and tries to pull me back into a horizontal position.

"I bought it at the chapel. The biggest they had, as you demanded."

"I...demanded?" I blink at him and then at the ring. The idea of me actually asking for something this ridiculous is frankly... well, stupid. My tastes tend to be more understated.

"You did," he says. "Right after you dared me to marry you."

He's fully laughing at me now, and I'm pretty sure my face is twisted in horror.

"I did what?!" My voice is more squeak than anything else. "You should never listen to drunk Rys—ever."

"Rys," Cas says, a little more sober now. "It wasn't real. Promise."

"Oh my God." My heart is beating so fast I wonder if I'm too young to have some sort of cardiac event.

I swing my legs over the side of the bed and let go of the sheet in favor of grabbing the large button-down on the floor that must be Cas's from last night. I pull it on even though it smells like alcohol and smoke. It'll have to do for now. I start rooting around the floor for my purse until I finally find it kicked halfway under the bed. My phone is dead when I pull it out.

"Rys," Cas says again. He's up and out of bed, almost naked and very distracting. "You okay?"

I stare down at my dead phone and have to talk myself out of crying. I swallow instead and stare at the wall hoping for a solution to this dilemma. I got married.

"Will you please put some clothes on? You look too…" I can't finish the sentence. He looks delicious, and even when I'm freaking out, I'd like him to kiss me and maybe for him to remind me what we did on our wedding night…okay, I have to stop myself before I do, or say, something more stupid.

With a little more confidence, I ask, "Can you lend me your phone charger? I can't believe you had sex with a drunk woman."

"I…we didn't have sex." He pulls on a shirt from his luggage and then grabs a cord from one of his bags and he tosses it to me. I sit on the couch in the adjoining room to plug the phone in. He brings me a clean t-shirt and some gym shorts with a corded waist.

"Where's my weekender bag?"

He shrugs. "We lost it somewhere in the hotel. I asked the concierge to search for it."

I narrow my gaze. "So I'm naked, but we didn't have sex. Mind explaining how that happened?"

"You gave me a show"—he scans the bedroom—"since we didn't have a bachelor or bachelorette party."

"What does that mean?"

"You said we should go to the strip club to celebrate. While we argued, you concluded that if we didn't go there, you'd bring the fun to me and...well, it happened. After you finished, you fell asleep, but not before I convinced you to put a pair of boxer briefs on."

"God, I've never..."

"Done that before." He nods. "You repeated that at least five times while we were about to get married."

"I said it?"

He nods a couple of times. "I can call the concierge to check on your bag," he says after I change. The shorts are comically large. "They can pick up something from a nearby store."

I frown at him. "You can do that?"

He shrugs. "I can get anything you need, babe."

The tone in how he says it melts my heart. I wish I had someone who'd do anything for me. Not that a man like that exists. Maybe my mother is right, and there's no such thing as perfect love, and what if I choose to be alone?

"Rys?" He gives me a worrisome look.

"Okay," I mumble.

He chuckles but nods as he picks up the hotel room phone and dials a number. It's amazing how fast he can get someone to bring me some clothes and charge everything to the room.

"Thanks," I say after he hangs up. "I don't think I'm up to doing a real walk of shame today."

When I pick up my phone, the level of notifications lighting it up as it boots makes me frown again. "I have a social media account?"

He smirks. "You might."

"Why would I do that?" I grumble at the phone as I unlock it and decide what to tackle first.

"Uh," Cas interrupts before I can open any of the texts. I look up to see him hovering awkwardly in the doorway with his own cell. I do not like how shaken he looks at all. "Fuck. We might have a little problem."

What now?

Chapter Eighteen

Caspian

As if summoned by hell itself, Gatsby barges into the hotel room without even a knock to announce himself. I'm fleetingly grateful that Rys is dressed. I'm not even given a moment to rebuke Gatsby for intruding before he's off to the races.

"Do you know what you've done?" his voice booms throughout the room.

I rear back as he comes within striking distance of me. I cross my arms and glare at him. We've never hit each other, and I hope he doesn't try because he'll be the one knocked unconscious.

"What were you thinking?"

Before I can say anything, he holds up a hand to stop me. "No, don't answer that," he snaps. "You weren't thinking."

"Um," Rys interrupts with raised eyebrows.

Gatsby notices her for the first time. If anything, his expression grows even darker.

"Was this your idea?" he asks her. "It must have been, right? You wanted your fifteen minutes of fame?"

This time, I do clap my brother on the shoulder. "Never talk to her like that," I warn him. "And explain what's going on."

He takes a step back, studies us both, and sighs.

"What's going on is you two lovebirds livestreamed your fucking wedding last night, and it's on every sports blog and network show in the world."

Rys looks completely shell-shocked. She stares open-mouthed at him and then looks at me.

"Livestreamed…what?" she asks faintly. "You said it was a joke, not…people know about this? Is this the little problem you were talking about?"

"No. I saw a text from him that he was heading this way, but I didn't know." I glare at him, clearing my throat as I try to assimilate the words he just said. "I'm sorry, livestreamed?"

He nods.

It's my turn to look a little dumbfounded at my brother. He's scowling at the both of us and tapping at his phone, no doubt informing Lysander and Aslan that he's here.

"Sit down," he orders both Rys and me.

We obey like schoolchildren who know they're in for a lecture. Absurdly, I grab Rys's hand and hold it, but she snatches it away, pulling up her legs and hugging them.

Gatsby places his phone screen up on the coffee table in front of Rys and me. He taps the play button, and the tinny music from the chapel is immediately recognizable. I frown at the footage. Had I given my phone to someone? I don't remember—wait, I did give it to someone to take a few pictures.

How had I not noticed the rest of this?

"Congratulations, you made SportsNet this morning. They've been wedging this video between analysis of the games from last night."

I run a hand over my face.

"Fuck," I drawl out the word long and low. "I need to call Lang."

"It's a joke, though, right?" Rys says from beside me.

Gatsby taps the phone. "Does that look like a joke, sweetheart?"

She leans forward to watch the video of herself laughing alongside me at an almost neon-pink altar. I'm just thankful the video-taker is far enough away that our actual words aren't on the video, just our laughing as we take the vows a very old Elvis gives us. "So it can't be that big of a deal?"

"A joke?" Gatsby asks.

I nod. "We were just fooling around. Nothing legal. Just some fun."

"Well, have fun explaining that to the millions, if not billions of people who've seen it. By tomorrow everyone in the world is going to know about your nuptials. And it's only a matter of time before they know who she is too, so you've got a shitstorm coming." He looks over to Rys and squints at her. "Who are you, by the way?"

Rys soundlessly opens and closes her mouth a few times. She seems too shocked to process what's happening, and I don't blame her.

"Her name is Rys." I clear my throat. "She's the girl who came to the vineyard with Benedict a few years ago. I recall telling you about her. We ran into each other last night after she had a bad night. We were just...blowing off some steam."

"You blow off steam by having sex, not streaming a fake wedding," he growls.

Rys's phone vibrates on the table where it's still tethered to my charger. The screen says "MOM," and her face falls when she sees who is calling.

"Fuck," she mutters, ignoring the call.

"Not ready to tell your family about the joyful nuptials?" Gatsby's sarcastic tone makes me want to punch him.

"I need more information before I talk to her."

Her phone vibrates twice again while Gatsby walks us through the epic shitstorm that has whipped up since last night. The ceremony was livestreamed to the millions of followers on my social media, then shared several thousand more times until it trended on Twitter and got picked up by the networks. In a few words, my reputation as a quiet, private guy who just wants to put pucks in the net, is basically blown to bits.

As if summoned by my sheer dismay, my agent calls.

"Hey, Lang," I answer and then put the phone on speaker. "I'm here with Gatsby and Rys. She's the one in the video."

"Your wife?" he barks. "I swear...never a dull moment with my clients. I'm on my honeymoon, and you...fuck you. Seriously."

"It was a joke."

There's a long exhale on the other side of the phone, and I can practically see Lang pinching the bridge of his nose.

"So, was it a joke when you called my assistant and told him to make sure he filed the marriage license first thing in the morning?"

"What the fuck are you talking about?"

"You called my assistant and left a message."

"Yes, to make sure that he had someone pick up the license and get rid of it, not file it. Fuck!"

"Well, congratulations to you and Mrs. Caspian Spearman. You need a bodyguard for her."

"Why?" Rys gasps.

I wince. "Sorry, I didn't think this would happen."

"The wedding or the livestream?" Lang asks dryly, which makes my brother snort.

"So the wedding isn't a joke?" Rys almost stutters. "My life is over."

My mouth thins. Being married to me can't be that big of a deal or so torturous.

"We could do a few things," Lang says, ignoring her comment. "We should start by locking down every social media you have and don't breathe a word of any of this to anyone outside of your most trusted people. The only thing worse than a drunk wedding is a livestreamed wedding meant as a joke involving your well-known rival's girlfriend. I mean, what the fuck, Cas?"

Rys gasps. "How do you know?"

"It's my job to know everything, sweetheart. What the ever-loving fuck you two were thinking is beyond me, but we'll spin this and make it right."

Rys clears her throat before I can rally a response. "I under-stand the lockdown and everything, but shouldn't we clarify that we aren't married and get an annulment?"

"No," Lang says. "That will only make it worse. People will rip *you* to shreds. It already looks bad. You're lucky no one has tracked down that douchebag Roderick yet, by the way. I'm sure he'll have some truly charming thoughts on this."

Rys squeaks like she hadn't even thought about her now ex-boyfriend. A small part of me feels satisfied that he was so thor-oughly off her mind until now. That had been the whole point of last night, after all.

"So, what? Do we pretend we got married? How is that any kind of endgame?"

"Let me repeat this. *You two are married.* Please, don't confirm anything. You deny nothing. Cas, you simply say 'no comment' when asked anything personal beyond your performance in the latest game, okay? We'll have a plan set in a few days. I have to talk to all the public relations people I know to see how we salvage this shitshow. You two figure out where home is and... stay put."

"And what? Rys puts her life on hold for months?" I ask.

"It's that or throw her to the sharks, Cas," Lang says. "Think about how the WAGs are already treated, and now think about how not only they'll react to Rys, but also the public reaction. Right now, it looks like you stole another player's girlfriend from under his nose and married her while laughing your heads off. It doesn't play well in any light. How in the world you ended up with a stranger in bed is beyond me."

"We met before," I say. "At the vineyard. She's a family friend."

"Okay, I can work with that. There's a backstory. The best way to play this is if we pretend you two are in a legitimate, loving relationship that just happened to move very quickly. Two old flames who happened to find each other at just the right time."

Rys lets out a very long exhale and then uncoils herself from the couch. She paces the floor behind the couch and runs a hand through her still messy hair.

"This is…a lot," she says. "I think I need some air."

After she goes to the room and closes the door, Gatsby looks at me. "We can always get rid of her."

"No. We need to protect her," I say with a warning voice.

"So I heard you right," Lang interrupts. "We *do* care about this Rys. I mean, it's clear in one of the videos. The way you look at her—it's not lust, but—"

"The video I saw can't give you that. It's blurry and—"

"Do you think that's the only one? At least five different people recorded and posted original content. Thankfully no one has linked her to her ex yet…but someone will, and I want to get ahead of that curve. Can I trust that you'll lie low?"

"Of course. About getting some security for her—"

"On it."

"Sorry for ruining your honeymoon."

"No worries. Six weeks vacationing is giving me a rash," Lang jokes. "I needed something to do. We'll figure this out."

"Pack your shit. We're going home," Gatsby orders.

"I—"

"You're due to leave today anyway. We'll take her to Paradise Bay or Santa Cruz. From there, you can decide what's next."

Chapter Nineteen

Rys

I LEAVE Cas and his brother to hash out more things with his agent. At first, I just pace around the bedroom, trying to sort through my thoughts. I purposely leave my phone out on the coffee table. More so when I know why everyone in my life has decided to text me. I wince again, thinking about my mom calling twice. She'll have a lot to say, and I'm not looking forward to it.

How am I going to explain to her that I got married by mistake?

Oops I was drunk, and the guy who was supposed to stop this misunderstood my now husband's voicemail. That's an explanation she's not going to accept.

The lecture is going to be so much fun—not.

Things like this only happen to me. I went from being the pretend girlfriend of a star hockey player to becoming the wife of his rival.

Way to go, Rys!

Oh God…what's going to happen to my job? Nothing. No one will care who I'm married to or what I do with my free time. I'm just a vet—a simple, boring veterinarian.

Cas's fans won't even glance at me. I'm a veterinarian, for God's sake. I adore my job, but there's nothing exciting about what I do. My four-legged clients won't care about my marital status.

I'm debating if the room phone would be safe to call my sister from, and at least loop her into this madness, when Cas knocks on my door. He has a few paper bags that he holds out a little sheepishly. Oh, the clothes. I'd forgotten about them in all the madness. I take them gratefully.

"Thanks," I say as I peek into the slim, black La Perla bag. I notice soft neutral brown and some blue silk. I probably don't even want to look at the price tags, but the fabrics are incredibly soft to the touch. The other bag has a nice pair of leggings, a tank top, and a tie-waist white blouse. "This looks great."

Cas looks around the room before clearing his throat. "Sorry. I—I swear I called so they wouldn't file the paperwork. I don't know what happened."

"We could say it was a joke."

"Give me a few days to figure this out."

"Your people, you mean?"

He gives me a shy smile. "Yeah."

I could call Leyla. Maybe her sister-in-law could help us.

Doesn't she work for the Orcas since her husband owns the team? I gasp and cover my mouth. She knows. My boss knows.

"Everything okay?"

"I… Do you know the Aldridges?"

He nods slowly, giving me a questioning look.

"My boss…she owns the animal clinics where I work."

His brows shoot up. "Wait, Leyla Aldridge is your boss?"

"Yeah," I whisper, then swallow hard.

He grins. "You work at the vet clinic close to the arena. We can date when I'm in town."

Is he serious? "Can we focus on our current issue?"

"Listen. This will quiet down soon. No one will remember us by the end of Wednesday. For now, you and I are going to San Fran—"

"Why?"

"To chill while we figure out what we're going to do. We might stay at my apartment or go to Santa Cruz with my older sister, Fern."

"Why?"

He gives me a look as if saying *do you know any other words*, but then smiles, and in a soothing tone says, "No one will know we're there, and it'll be easy to figure out what we're going to do afterward. If we could stay married for a little while though…"

Cas doesn't finish the sentence. I wonder if his career is in jeopardy? Or… I don't know what can happen to him, but I say, "I'll do it. Whatever you need me to do to play along. Let's be married for a few days."

How hard can it be? It's not like the time Britney Spears married her old friend for twenty-four hours. Even that blew up, and no one even remembered the incident after a couple of years.

He looks a little gobsmacked. I smile, reaching out to poke him in the side. "Besides, it's not like the sex is that bad," I add because I know it will ruffle his feathers.

"That bad?" He huffs at me.

"Tolerable at best," I say as seriously as I can, barely holding back laughter.

He looks so affronted that I can't help the giggle that escapes me. A moment later, I find myself scooped over his shoulder and thrown onto the bed. He leans over me, huge and looming, with one thick arm on either side of me.

"You don't have to do anything, you know," he says softly. "We can say it's a joke, and I'll take all the blame. You can just go on with your life."

"You know that's not how it would go," I sigh.

I hate to admit his agent and his brother are right. Public opinion tends to blame the woman in any given situation. "Besides, who's to say I don't have my own reasons for wanting to pretend to be married for a while?"

He raises a playful eyebrow at me and pulls a hand suggestively up my shirt to stroke at my bare skin.

"The sex?" he asks.

"Obviously." I laugh and then push him away.

"So it was great," he continues.

"There's that," I agree, not even trying to lie anymore. Sex with Cas was great and easy. We could try again. At least with him, I know what to expect. "Also, my mother will expect more than a mistaken-drunken-public wedding."

"Your mother?"

"She...has some strong views about the institution of marriage," I say, choosing my words carefully. "Let's just say that if I were to announce this wedding was annulled or whatever, she would be crowing about how terrible men and marriage are for the rest of my existence."

"Huh," he says.

"Yeah." I pat him on the arm and then slide off the bed, out from under him. I put my hands on my hips and grab the new clothes from where they've fallen. "Now, get out of here while I change. Is your brother still here?"

Cas nods. "He's waiting for us so we can drive to the airport."

I guess this whole sham has begun. All I can do is hope that we can keep this up for whatever length they need us to do it.

Chapter Twenty

Rys

My phone rings just as I'm unplugging it. It's Milly. I stare at it and then at Cas.

"Is everything okay?"

I shake my head. Nothing has been okay since I boarded a plane to Vegas. This might be cataloged as the worst trip in my entire life. "It's my sister," I mumble.

"Why don't you answer." He squeezes my hand reassuringly.

"We have to go," Gatsby growls.

Cas glares at him. "She has to talk to her family."

"Fine but make it fast."

The call goes to voicemail, but instead of letting that go, I call her back. I might as well get this over with now.

"You got married?" she screeches before I can say hello.

"Hello to you too."

"You. Got. Married!"

"Maybe?"

She groans. "There's no maybe. I watched the whole thing." She pauses. "Twice. Some woman you don't know was your maid of honor. Not me—your sister. And where's Thad in all this mess? I thought this weekend you two were finally going to fuck."

"It's a long story."

"Start from the beginning."

"Milly, I don't have time," I say, hoping she'll let me go. "We have to—"

"I need something. Mom's been calling me all morning," she interrupts me. "I don't care if the puppy of the president needs you. We have to talk now."

What a coincidence. Mom has been calling me too. I just won't answer the phone. Though, what do I tell Milly?

"I mean, I get why you did it," she interrupts the silence.

"You do?" Because honestly, I can't even remember what I did last night.

"Yes. You still love *him*."

Okay, she lost me.

Why do people insist that I was in love with Thad?

I liked the idea of us, but nothing happened since he was just using me to book him rooms and…asshole. Of course, I play stupid in front of my sister. "I'm in love with who exactly?"

"Caspian Spearman. He's the weekend guy. You told me."

"I—"

"It's okay to admit it. He's your husband," she interrupts me, again.

It was a great weekend but I didn't fall in love with him. I dreamt of the possibilities though, but I wouldn't go that far.

"He's not—"

"Rys, it's fine," she cuts me off. "I just can't believe you didn't wait for me. I'm hurt."

And you know what, she doesn't get to play the victim. "You did the same, eloped and just let everyone know that you finally got married—via text. I was roped with your children for the weekend while you were on your honeymoon in Cozumel."

"It was different," the cunning bitch argues.

"Probably because I didn't reject my boyfriend and the father of my children for years. Not that I have either one of them," I clarify.

"I can't believe you're throwing that in my face when you should be ashamed of getting married in front of Elvis and anyone with a phone or a computer." She huffs.

"Me...you know what, I don't have time."

"We have to talk about your wedding and your plans, or I'll have to block Mom, and I can't since she's going to be watching the kids this week. I can't avoid her," she almost whimpers.

The brat. I love her, but she's always thinking about number one.

"No, we don't. I'll call you when I can, which might be between now and never," I say, and I wish I could just hang up the phone loudly so she could feel my irritation.

"Everything okay?" Cas gives me a worried look.

Gatsby shakes his head. "Family, you love them, but they're a pain in the ass. We have to go. Please don't talk to anyone, not even your family about the situation. Not until you two have a solid story."

"I get it, his career matters, but my family is concerned. I can't just be incommunicado until the end of time."

"It's not just his..." Gatsby turns to Cas. "She doesn't know who we are, does she?"

Cas shakes his head.

I'm the one who says, "Up until six months ago, I had no idea he was a hockey player."

Gatsby glares at him. "What the fuck?"

"When we met, she treated me like a normal person. I didn't want to break the illusion by telling her who I am."

"And yet, you tattooed Polaris for her?" Gatsby rolls his eyes. "I'll never understand you, kid."

I ignore the tattoo comment and say, "So what if you're a hockey player? It's not like I'm a puck bunny."

"I own part of Spearman LP and the vineyard," he says.

Gatsby nods as if understanding, then looks at me. "Most women are attracted to our checkbooks, not us. Some of us have had bad experiences—like him. I understand why you'd be upset though."

"From my perspective, you were a breath of fresh air. Someone who was hanging out with me for me, and not my status." Cas smiles, his thumb smoothing my forehead. "I like this little angry frown of yours. It's cute, just like you."

"Don't try to—"

"I will make it up to you. Don't you think I regret not getting your number or telling you who I was? I regretted it for years. This time, I promise to be transparent."

Before I can tell him there's no this time or things won't go further from a few months of pretending that we're together, his brother says, "Let's get home. My people and Aslan's are looking into this PR mess too."

There are so many people involved, and yet, I have to keep quiet.

How big is this mess though?

Chapter Twenty-One

Caspian

GATSBY LEARNS THAT EVERYONE, including Maia and Soleil, are at Fern and Elliot's house. I usually don't mind going to Santa Cruz to visit my family, but I don't think it's a good idea to introduce Rys to everyone while she's under so much stress.

My family can be a handful. I love them dearly, but the triplets, Gatsby, Aslan, and Lysander, get too fatherly and begin micromanaging me. Gatz has already started, and Aslan will take over as soon as he sees me. Then there's my sister Fern, who's a mother hen.

Heath might be at the hospital and won't give a shit about what's happening to me until later. Cory, the littlest of the Spearmans, is nosy as fuck. She's going to be inquisitive and annoy my girl before I finish introducing Rys to the family.

"Ready?" I ask, holding her hand.

"No, but it doesn't seem like I have any other option."

I take her into my arms, resting my hands on the small of her back. "Look at me, Rys."

She lifts her head, and her eyes find mine. "I promise that no matter what, this is going to be okay."

"You can't say that."

"I can, because I'll make sure that nothing touches you. My agent and family might be concerned about me, but my number one priority is you."

"It shouldn't be," she mumbles.

Looking at her, holding her closer to me, and feeling the warmth of her body makes me finally do it. Kiss her. My lips meet hers. It's meant to be a peck on the lips, but when I feel the mouth I've been missing for so long, I can't help but devour her. I want to kiss every part of her, take her with me. Never let her go. We already had a great moment, and I thought it was the only one we'd share, but now I want more—an infinite beat that will last us a lifetime.

But of course, Gatsby has to go and interrupt us. "Can we do this another time?"

I groan, and Rys laughs for the first time since we woke up this morning. That melodic sound gives me the hope that things will be okay.

"Ready?"

She nods, and that's precisely when the front door of Fern's house opens. "So…it's all a lie, huh?" Lysander looks from Rys to me.

Love him, but sometimes he drives me crazy. "What the fuck are you talking about?"

"What happens in Vegas..." He glances at Rys. "Didn't stay in Vegas. I see her, and she looks hotter than the last time she visited the vineyard."

"I don't have the bandwidth to deal with you," I say with a warning voice. "Where is everyone?"

"Outside. Fern's only a few weeks away from popping and you had to stress the shit out of her. She's not happy," he says the last words in a singsong tone.

My heart almost stops. "Is she okay?" I don't wait for him to answer. I run toward the patio where everyone sits and find her snuggled against her husband. "Fern, are you okay?"

"Oh hey, it's the newlywed. I guess the invitation got lost in the mail," she says, rolling her eyes. "Where's your bride?"

My heart almost stops. How could I forget Rys?

"Fuck. Lysander told me you were stressed out, and I...let me get her."

When I arrive at the foyer, Rys is waiting next to Gatsby and Lysander.

"A veterinarian?" Lysander crosses his arms. "Why in the world would you marry a jock? You spent your entire life studying, and now you're with stupid? Is it because we have money? She should sign a prenup."

What the fuck is he doing? I pull her to me before glaring at him. "Shut the fuck up!"

"Oh, he's here." He shrugs. "Oops, was I not supposed to bring up the obvious."

"You're an asshole."

He shakes his head. "I'm not the one who married the first chick who—"

I set Rys behind me. "Say one more word and I swear—"

"Stop," Gatsby orders and glares at Lysander. "I know you think you're funny, Lysander, but right now, he doesn't need your shit. We brought them here so they can have a moment of peace before heading to Portland."

Lysander sighs. "I don't like this."

Rys moves away from my protection, and the little thing is

right in front of him, puffed chest and chin up. "You think I'm enjoying it? I worked hard to be who I am, and tomorrow, I might get fired. Helping animals is my passion. I don't need your brother's money or his fame."

"Let's go, babe. I'm going to introduce you to my family."

"What about me? You can start with your favorite brother," Lysander protests.

We make our way toward the patio, but I say, "Until you apologize to her, you're just an asshole who happens to have the same face as Aslan and Gatz."

Before opening the sliding door, I kiss her temple. "Are you okay?"

"I'm trying, but visiting your family is…"

"They're not bad," I promise.

Her big brown eyes stare at me. "I don't care about your money. If you need me to sign something—"

"Nope. I need you to ignore Lysander. He's in protector mode. Remember I told you about Dad's death and how my three oldest brothers became like our fathers?"

She nods.

"This is them protecting me. I might need to remind them several times that they have to respect you and that I'm not a child."

"So, I should expect number three to do the same?" Her shoulders slump.

"Probably worse, but I'll stop Aslan before he opens his mouth."

"This… I didn't—"

"I know." I kiss the tip of her nose.

"It was—"

"I know." I give her a peck on her mouth.

"Do you?"

"Yes. You didn't do this on purpose, but my family is wondering. I was in charge of taking care of you, and instead of keeping you safe, I pushed you to the social media piranhas— and my family."

"I feel responsible too. You know what they say. It takes two to tango."

I take her into my arms. "I promise this won't affect you. I'll do everything in my power to ensure your life doesn't implode."

"That's a tall order."

"Trust me." I soften my tone, pulling her even closer to me.

"I've only seen you two times in my life," she reminds me.

"And sometimes that's all people need to know someone's soul. I think I'm pretty familiar with yours."

She narrows her gaze. "For a hockey player, you're pretty smooth."

I smirk because I don't know how to respond. I've only felt this way with her, no one else.

Chapter Twenty-Two

Rys

I WANT to crawl into my skin when I step outside the house and six sets of eyes are on me. "Everyone, meet your new sister-in-law Rys…" Cas looks at me.

A guy who I assume is Aslan since he looks a lot like Lysander and Gatsby shakes his head and says, "Why am I not surprised that you don't know your wife's last name."

"Rys Holland," I mumble.

"If you want to make this believable, you have to get to know her better," Gatsby says as he walks toward a woman who sits in a rocking chair cradling a baby. "Hey, my Little Sun, did you miss me?"

He gently grabs the baby, kissing the top of her head and then the woman who held the infant. "How's my beautiful wife?"

She smiles. "We're doing well."

"Can we go back to Rys?" A guy who sits in the back corner looks at me. His brows rise in amusement. "Rys Holland. I can't believe you don't know your wife's last name. God, you really like to play the dumb card, don't you?"

"Shut up, doc."

The guy walks close to me. "Hey, I'm Heathcliff. Everyone calls me Heath. Welcome to the madness."

I smile and wave with my fingers. "Hi. I'm just here temporarily."

"Okay, you met the doctor. He's younger than me." Caspian points at the pregnant lady sitting on the big couch. "That's my sister Fern. She's about to pop with two children. Next to her is my brother-in-law, Elliot. The tall guy who is identical to Lysander and Gatsby is Aslan, and next to him is his wife, Keaton. Maia is Gatz's wife and the brains of the duet, and the baby is our niece, Soleil."

I bow my head slightly. "It's nice to meet you all."

"Where are Cory and Hux?" Cas asks.

Aslan checks his watch. "They should be here soon. Can you tell us more about yourself?"

Caspian's phone rings. He pulls it out and shows it to me. *Agent from hell.* He waves it and says, "Lang's calling. We have to take this."

Caspian

I take Rys's hand and walk toward the library, where I shut the door and answer.

"What do you have for us?"

"I spoke to Hadley Aldridge—"

"No," Rys gasps. "Am I fired?"

Lang chuckles. "No, but Leyla wants you to call her as soon as possible. She's concerned about you. Hadley and I agreed that living in Portland would be the safest. You'll have security and family close by."

"My father lives in Vermont and my mother in Austin." Rys pauses for a second. "As far as I know, Caspian's family lives in Northern California."

Lang sighs. "I meant the Orcas. Mills Aldridge treats everyone like family. Plus, Leyla and your colleagues are there for you. That means that even if Caspian is out of town, there'll be someone to check up on you. As I mentioned, there'll be security twenty-four seven. I'm cashing in a favor, Caspian, don't fuck this up, or I'll drop your ass."

Rys gives me a concerned look. "Why do we have security? I don't understand."

"I told you, I'm going to make sure that nothing happens to you."

Lang clears his throat. "Tomorrow, Hadley will explain her plan—she's working on it. If you need anything, call me, but I already emailed you the numbers for the security company in case you need their assistance."

The knots on my back finally loosen up. "Thank you, Lang."

"That's what you pay me for," he says before ending the conversation.

When I turn to look at Rys, she's hugging herself and staring at the floor. "Are you okay?"

"I'm trying," she mumbles.

"If you want us to go to Portland now…" I glance at the door. "My family can be intimidating."

She's sucking on her bottom lip, and then, when she looks at me, says, "I'm pretty sure they hate me."

"Nah. My brothers are trying to figure out your angle. They can't understand why you'd marry me without knowing me."

"Did they do the same with your sisters- or brother-in-law?"

"It was different. Keaton has been a part of Aslan's life for years. Maia was Gatz's college sweetheart, and Elliot was friends with the triplets before he and Fern..." I whistle. "That was a mess, but they love each other, and they're happy. I guess you're the first unfamiliar face."

"A lot has happened since the last time I saw you," she says.

"Well, you shouldn't have left, and you would know everything." I show her my phone. "I'm still waiting for your call to let me know that you arrived safe at your destination."

She gives me an apologetic smile. "Clearly I should've; next time I might do it."

"I recommend you stick around for a little longer." I wink at her.

"How long?"

"Maybe for—"

Lysander barges inside the library. "We're waiting for you, dinner is ready."

"Can you knock on the door?"

"I could, but I don't want to," he answers.

He's trying my patience. "What do you want?"

"As I mentioned, dinner is ready. Shall we?"

Rys looks at me and then at him.

"Hey, it's going to be okay," I say reassuringly.

"I want to believe you, but I can't see how this won't end in disaster."

I kiss her hard, reassuringly. Nothing can go wrong as long as we stay on top of everything, right?

Chapter Twenty-Three

Rys

WHEN WE LAND IN PORTLAND, we're met by a man wearing a suit. "Hello, Caspian," he greets him. "Heard you need our services."

"Seth?" Cas looks around. "Did your cousin send you to break my legs?"

Seth laughs and shakes his head. "Nah. Jude's not like that."

"So why are you here?"

Seth extends his hand. "You must be Rys Holland. It's a pleasure to meet you, Ms. Holland. I'm Seth Bradley."

"Hi," I answer, staring at his gray eyes.

"So why are you here?" Cas asks again.

"Lang asked me to lend you some guys." He glances at Rys. "I just came to take you home, give you some instructions, and head back to Seattle."

"Thank you, I appreciate it."

"I'm sure you'll change your mind when you get the bill, but let's not sour the happy nuptials." He points at a black SUV with tinted windows. "Shall we?"

Once in the car, I whisper, "You have bodyguards?"

I have many other questions, like who is Jude?

Cas shakes his head. "They're for you."

"I don't need protection," I whisper-shout. "Who's going to care about a harmless veterinarian?"

"We don't know, but I want to ensure no one will get close to you."

"I'll be fine."

He lifts my hand, kisses my knuckles, and says, "Do this one little thing for me, please."

"I'm in the middle of the last favor you asked of me. Remember when I agreed to stay married to you?"

"I thought you were doing it for your mom."

My entire body sags. I keep sending Mom to voicemail. I'm tempted to ask his public relations person or his agent to give me an official statement for her. "Well, that too."

"Which one is it?"

"Both?"

He shakes his head. "Either way, I need them to keep an eye on you."

"I'll be fine," I assure him.

"What if something happens? Like a fan trying to scratch you because you snatched me away from her?"

Can that happen? "Maybe I should just disappear?"

"No." His voice comes out like a growl. "You're staying with me."

"Why?"

"Because I already lost you once, Rys. I won't let that happen again, not without a fight."

"What?" Who is he fighting? Did I miss something?

"Never mind."

"No, you were saying something," I insist.

"It's not as important as discussing your security."

"We're here," Seth says, and I realize we're slightly outside the city, close to the woods. The house is almost as big as Fern's. Though instead of looking like a Mediterranean villa, it looks like a cabin—a big cabin in the middle of the woods.

"I thought you said you live in Portland."

"Lake Oswego is only twenty minutes from downtown," he says. "Come on, let me show you the place. You're going to love it. Elliot designed it and built it."

Seth is already opening the door. "Time for you to go and face the party."

"Party?" Cas arches an eyebrow.

Seth grins. "Mills and his wife are waiting for you. The clothing you requested is in the master bedroom, and the bill from the concierge service will be emailed to you tomorrow morning."

"Thank you," Caspian mumbles.

Seth salutes me. "It was nice meeting you. Let us know if there's something we can do for you."

We watch Seth leave. I take in the entire property. Trees, fence, and maybe there's a lake on the other side of the house. He might say this is twenty minutes from Portland, but it feels like we're in a different state. We walk toward the main door. The stained-glass door is a work of art and fits perfectly with the siding.

When we enter, I freeze.

"Everything okay?" Cas asks.

No, I almost say when I spot not only Mills Aldridge but

Hadley, his wife, in the living room, but they're not alone. Leyla and her husband are here too.

"Rys." Leyla walks toward me and hugs me. "Are you okay?"

"Of course," I lie.

She's here to fire me. It's over.

Leyla saunters to where I stand and puts her hands on my shoulders. "I'm going to ask again, and this time I need you to tell me the truth. Are you okay?"

"Overwhelmed," I mutter.

"I'd be too if I got married in Vegas." She glances at Cas. "And not to my current boyfriend. What happened?"

"Can we start with that?" Hadley says and smiles at me. "Hey, Rys."

"Hi, how are you?"

She gives me her signature smile. "Good. Okay, for the next twenty minutes, I will be the Orcas' social media and public relationships director. Not your friend, okay."

I nod.

"There's a rumor that you were dating Roderick." She clears her throat. "Which I've kept as *just a rumor*. What happened with him? I thought you said things were going great—better."

I brief her on what happened with him. When I'm done with the story, her mouth opens in astonishment, and her face becomes red. "That asshole, I'm going to—"

"Babe, no," Mills Aldridge says. "We know what happens when you get upset."

"Did you hear what he did to her?"

"Yes, but we can't just—"

"Oh yes, I can. There are accounts to denounce cheaters. I wish we had proof."

"I have a video of them with the whole thing," I say, pulling out my phone.

Her face brightens. "You do?"

"I was hoping to capture his surprised face when he saw that I came to visit, but…"

"You were the one who got to be surprised?" Hadley's voice softens.

"Exactly."

Mills then looks from Cas to me. "And how did you two end up getting married?"

"I went to the bar—"

"She was distraught," Cas interrupts me. "I wanted to ensure she was okay, but one thing led to another, and things got a little out of hand."

"Lang filled me in on the miscommunication with his former assistant," Hadley chimes in.

"Former?" I ask, almost afraid that the man has lost his job.

"He fired him," Hadley says, then points at Pierce, who's been watching our exchange. "He's actually suing him. If the guy who's supposed to cover for you makes this mistake, you can't keep him on your payroll. So you two know each other?"

Cas tells her how we met.

"Oh, this is winery guy? The one who was soooo good in bed?" Leyla asks excitedly.

I glare at her. She shrugs. "Oops."

Cas's cocky smirk appears instantly. "Winery guy?"

"Focus on this issue, Caspian," I redirect his attention. I don't want him to know I've told everyone about him.

"Okay, I think I have the spin," Hadley says, rubbing her hands together. "I'm going to post a picture on the team's social media wishing you the best in the next step of your life. I'll call Rys Cas's longtime girlfriend. We'll say you two have been together since the winery incident."

"No one has seen us together," I remind her.

"And that's fine. He's a private guy." She looks at Caspian. "You've been able to keep everything secret until now that you finally made her your wife."

"How about all the people who know I was with Roderick?" I ask.

She grins. "You're good friends with him. The rivalry

between the two is just a hoax. People will understand when they see the video of him with another woman."

"What video?" Leyla, Pierce, Cas, and I ask.

Hadley points at my phone. "I need you to send it to me."

"But that'll ruin his reputation."

"For five minutes. It's either him or you, Rys. He's about to play martyr and claim that our Cas stole the love of his life away. His fans, and Cas's, will remember you as a cheater. If we show the video of him with a married woman, it'll be forgotten soon.

"Unfortunately, we live in a world where men can do no wrong, and women are judged by every little thing they do, even the amount of makeup they wear when grocery shopping."

I send her the video and realize she had sent me several messages throughout the day. I feel bad, but maybe it was better to meet her in person.

"Okay, this is the first step. For now, stay in the house, enjoy the heated pool, and catch up with all the shows you've been ignoring because you're busy at the animal clinic," she says. "We'll update you on what we think should be next."

"They're paying too much attention to a hockey player and little old me," I complain.

"You're married to one of the favorite players in the league, Rys. Women hate you, and they'll try to find a way to make you look bad. My job is to ensure that his reputation remains squeaky clean and that you don't get hurt in the process. Please trust me."

"Okay."

Chapter Twenty-Four

Caspian

"WORD on the street is that you stole Roderick's girl," Spacey greets me at morning skate two days later. Of my two alternate captains, Spacey is by far my favorite, so I don't want to take a swing at him, but it is tempting for a brief flash. He must see it on my face because he holds both hands up in defense. "Whoa, whoa, whoa, I see we're not joking yet. Okay."

I run a hand down my face and do a few laps around the ice with him.

"It's not that," I say. "I've just been dodging media all morning. They won't take 'no comment' for an answer."

"So much for 'no soap operas,' huh?" Spacey snorts. "Those vultures love a good soapy dramafest way more than they want to talk about our lines for the game tonight."

I grunt in agreement. Hadley's plan isn't working as well as we thought. Roderick is claiming the guy in the video isn't him —and that he's been with Rys for years. Years.

"So, she's sticking around, then?" Spacey ventures again, more hesitantly, after a couple of drills go by and we're both getting water at the bench. I squirt him with a bottle but then shrug.

"Yeah, she is," I say.

It's not a lie, and besides, I've been practicing every possible question and answer with Hadley, Mills, and Rys since the morning we'd woken up to this mess. "Her name is Rys. Be nice to her."

"I'm always nice," Spacey says defensively. "Anyway, give me her number after practice so I can pass it on to Shelly."

"Tell her to be nice too," I grumble at him.

"Much less likely." He laughs.

Shelly is a vicious pixie of a woman who Spacey married at eighteen. She's both terrifying and probably Rys's best chance at an ally within the WAGs group. She's one of the few girlfriends with an outside job—she's an architect who's probably smarter than the entire Orcas' roster.

"I'll get it to you," I promise. I'd hoped he would ask, actually. I have to be careful about how Rys is introduced to the guys, and this is probably our best way in. "She…" I hesitate and clear my throat. "I think she could use a friend, so I'd really appreciate it."

Spacey claps me on the helmet before skating off and joining another drill.

Later, after the morning skate is over, my worst nightmare

appears in the form of Hadley. She's waiting for me before I even get my skate guards on. "Didn't we already discuss our plan?"

"No, that was just a start. Today, we have more to talk about."

I sigh and lean against my stick in the hallway as the other guys filter past. A few hit me on the back in what I will interpret as support. They've been strangely quiet with the chirps this morning which probably meant Spacey told them all to keep it to themselves for now.

"Can I hit the showers before this conversation?" I ask Hadley hopefully.

She smiles at me like I'm an adorable child asking to finger paint or something.

"You could if I could trust you not to escape through the window instead of talking to me," she says.

I purse my lips but don't argue. Instead, I grab a towel from the bench and at least wipe most of my sweat off. I lean back on my stick and wait for the hall to clear out. Hadley waves at the last assistant on their way down the tunnel before turning back to me with a sigh.

"You really fucked up this weekend, you know?" She's nice enough to make it sound like a question. "Listen, I've been on the phone with Lang this morning."

"You have?" I hadn't expected Lang to take any more time off from his honeymoon for me, but I guess the guy is a control freak.

"Yeah, with Roderick's declarations, we have to make some changes. How comfortable is Rys going to be on camera—with you?"

"We aren't doing media. You said that yesterday."

"Mm-hmm," Hadley agrees. "No pressers or anything. I agree with Lang on that front, but I do have an idea. We include a lot of the wives in our behind-the-scenes bits. We can work Rys in."

"Do you have to do it?"

She raises her perfectly drawn-on eyebrows at me.

"Why wouldn't we?" she asks. "I mean, hopefully she has more on-camera personality than you, but otherwise, it's perfectly normal."

She studies me. "Are you protecting her, or are you trying to keep her away from me?"

"Protecting her," I say with conviction. "I lost her once, but it won't happen again."

She smiles. "We thought so. This isn't just a marriage that will expire once the season is over, is it?"

"Not for me. I assume you know the story of Paradise Bay."

She nods.

"I let her go that time, but now…"

"But you don't know her," she argues.

"Sometimes you don't have to be in love to recognize your soul mate. Sometimes, you just have to take a chance and not let it go. This is it."

"Okay, we have to help you keep the media away and keep you from doing something stupid."

I smile sheepishly. "Probably."

"So, we add her to the WAGs and we find a way to protect her while we convince your fans that Rys is the woman of your dreams and they should ship you—not hate her."

"Is that even possible?"

"The beauty of social media is that you can make people believe anything you want."

"I'll have to ask her," I say. "I'm not sure she's ready to be back on camera. This whole thing has been…unexpected."

"No shit," Hadley says dryly. "I know you'd rather die than livestream a personal event, so we knew something was sideways the second it came out. We're happy to help smooth this over though, Cas. I know media isn't your forte, but I hope we've known each other long enough that you can trust me when I say this will help everyone."

I nod. "I do trust you. You and Mills have always been more than good to me."

"Okay, get lost. Now you're just sucking up." She swats at

me. "You have my number, so call as soon as you can get her on board, and I'll have a sit-down with her to figure out what she's comfortable with."

"You could call her. She's your friend."

"Yes, but this is your relationship and your career. This has to be handled between the two of you."

"Okay. I'm going to connect her with Shelly as well," I say.

Hadley nods. "I was about to suggest that. It would be nice to have someone else from the wives' group in at least one of these spots, so Rys seems like less of an outsider."

I exhale. This is strangely a relief, even though it will involve cameras and people in our space. At least the cameras will be very firmly in the control of people who want us to look good and know how to do it. I've seen Hadley and her team work wonders before.

It's not that I thought my team wouldn't have my back, but it's always hard to predict how things will go exactly. I'm still not sure if this is going to end soon, and with the playoffs coming up, the media might not let this go.

What else can I do?

Chapter Twenty-Five

Rys

MY LIFE IS A DRAMEDY, day five.

I don't even know if that's the right number.

Do I count Saturday when everything began or…

Anyway, it's Thursday and I'm either having a continuous nightmare where I'm married to Caspian Spearman and I can't leave my house unless I'm driven by Lincoln, my bodyguard, or

I got so drunk last Saturday that I married that man and now I'm trying to survive this stupid mistake.

Either way, I feel trapped in what would be a fairy tale for many.

Do I like Cas? He's thoughtful, caring, and even loving. He's been showering me with affection from the moment we stepped into his house. I'm trying to set up some boundaries, so I don't fall madly in love with him.

In my experience, it takes years, *years,* to stop needing his lips. He's making me want them again.

What's going to happen when I have to sign the divorce papers?

This is why I think it would've been a lot simpler if we got an annulment. According to all the research I did, they wouldn't have given it to us though. The excuse of being under the influence isn't valid since we filed the license the next day. The list of reasons why we had to file for divorce goes on and on.

But what am I going to do when I have to leave his house because it's over?

Not that I want this to end. I find being with him hopeful, calming, like I don't need to wait for better days. He's the day that can last forever. Those are scary thoughts. It's not like I don't believe in love but falling for someone like Cas might destroy me and leave me bitter like my mother.

Maybe we should establish a no-sex, no-kissing, no-contact policy. I should just move out of his luxurious home and back into my apartment. He can just hire a model who can pretend to be me. I'm busy brooding while searching for a lawyer who can help me at least get a prenup when my phone buzzes. It's a text from Cas.

Cas: Shelly Spackman is going to contact you.
Rys: Who?
Cas: Doug's wife—Spacey.
Rys: Why?
Cas: To help you with the WAGs.

Rys: Have you considered hiring a model to play the part of your wife?

Cas: Stop with that.

Rys: She'll be perfect for you. Tall, thin, and put together.

Cas: Why don't I keep my beautiful wife instead? I know, crazy, but I think it's a lot better than dealing with a stranger. I'm not into threesomes, only into you. You should lift that no-PDA policy.

Rys: That's not what I said.

Cas: I'll be home around five. In the meantime, miss me.

When I read his texts one more time, my heart flutters. He's a smooth talker. I want to believe that he likes me, but does he?

Shelly Spackman is tall, with nearly luminescent skin and long red nails. Her hair is a perfect balayage in a faded blonde, and she's dressed in ripped jeans and a crocheted midriff top. It's hard not to feel a little self-conscious sitting across from her in my own t-shirt, jeans, and hasty ponytail. I am extremely grateful I'd at least taken the time to put on some eyeliner and lip gloss before leaving the house. Otherwise, I might have just ducked out of the coffee shop before she'd seen me.

"Rule number one, stay off Twitter and most of the internet." Shelly sits across from me at a table tucked into the back corner of a fancy coffee shop that isn't far from Cas's house. She continues, "Rule number two, if you do go on the internet, don't reply to anything. Ever."

"I don't have a Twitter and just opened an Instagram this weekend, which I locked," I admit. She doesn't need to know Cas opened it because we were daring each other while I was super drunk.

She nods, like I've done something right even though it's mostly just that I was in vet school when Twitter got really big and I missed the boat, and now I'm too intimidated by it to try it out.

"Good," she says. "People will be looking for it. And when I say people, I mean rabid fangirls, and trust me, Cas has plenty. They'll want to dissect your every move for a while, especially since I don't think Cas has ever had a public girlfriend. Much less…well."

"A surprise wife?" I joke weakly. I kind of wish there was some Baileys in my coffee. I wonder if I should be worried how much this situation makes me want to drink.

"Exactly." Shelly's smile softens a little, like she might suspect where my mind is at the moment. "How's that all going, by the way?"

"Huh?"

Shelly rests her face in one hand and tilts it sideways, looking at me.

"Cas doesn't seem like the type who'd marry a girl overnight."

"We actually met a long time ago at his family's vineyard and have been dating on and off. With his schedule and mine…" I say, trying to remember what we agreed to tell people.

Is there an official statement? This is worse than a reality show. At least there the production team edits the scenes, here I don't have anyone to say cut and repeat.

I remember the vineyard story is part of our narrative, but are we supposed to say that we've been dating since we met or not?

Ugh, I need cue cards to keep the story straight. And before I make a fool of myself, I finish with, "Things just kind of happened in Vegas."

She taps her nails on the table and the way she's looking at me tells me she knows I'm not telling the entire truth. One side of her mouth tugs into a smile after a few more moments of scrutiny.

"Well, get used to people asking, is all I'm saying," she says. "Also… I wasn't sure if I should bring this up or not, but is it true you were dating Thad Roderick before this? My sources were strangely mixed."

"Your sources?"

"Wait, answer first." She wags a finger at me. "Sources later."

"Oh, right, yes," I exhale. "We were friends—no benefits. He needed someone to be his plus-one. It was harmless."

She nods and fires the next question. "What do you know about the video that's circulating? Is that him?"

I smile at her coyly. "I can't say anything about it. He's my friend."

"So, the girl in the video is his real girlfriend?"

I lean forward and whisper, "They used me so her husband wouldn't know that they're together."

"Ouch," Shelly sympathizes. "Some of these guys can be real scum about the women they date. Not Cas, as far as I can tell. He doesn't date much, of course, but I've never heard a bad word from anyone. He keeps his nose clean."

There's a heavily implied "until he married you out of the blue" in that last sentence, but there doesn't seem to be any malice behind it, just dry observation.

"I imagine he hates the limelight on him right now," Shelly says.

I nod, finally feeling like I'm on some firmer ground. I could talk about Cas easily enough.

"He's been on the phone with his agent and the Orcas' PR a lot," I admit. "I think they're all in agreement that he should avoid the media as much as possible, which is a relief for Cas."

"It's never really been his bag," she says. "And a few of the national media guys have a real nasty edge to their coverage on him."

"Can you tell me why?" I ask.

She shrugs and sips on her iced coffee for a moment. Her face scrunches in thought. "I really don't know, but Doug's theory is that since he's a rich kid, many think he bought his way into the league, which is a lie. He busts his ass on the ice—and he's done that since college."

I must look as overwhelmed as I feel, because she laughs and pats my hand.

"Don't worry, no tests on that later," she assures me. "You'll get a handle on the politics of everything eventually. Hockey pundits like to pretend it's all very complicated, but really they're just a bunch of overgrown kids squabbling with each other over obscene amounts of money."

Chapter Twenty-Six

Caspian

WHEN I ARRIVE HOME, the house is empty. I text Lincoln to check Rys's whereabouts. As predicted, she's still with Shelly. I head to the kitchen and begin preparing dinner for us. It's strange to come home and not just grab a meal from the freezer and nuke it as I often do when I'm in town.

As I open a bottle of wine, my beautiful wife enters the

kitchen. Fuck, I have a wife and it doesn't freak me out. Actually, it feels just right. If only I'd had the courage a few years back and looked for her, we wouldn't be in the middle of a clusterfuck.

"Hey, beautiful," I greet her, setting the bottle on the table. "Are you hungry?"

"Hi," she says with a soft voice.

She looks nervous, so I dare to ask, "How did it go today?"

"Shelly mentioned there wouldn't be a test." She smiles, and the way her eyes crinkle makes me hungry—for her.

I want to consume her. I've been waiting patiently for her to catch up, but maybe she needs a little push. Hinting that I want to devour her might not be enough. I can't believe I forgot she's reserved and, at times, self-conscious. That shell she wears is cute, but I like her a lot more when she comes out of it and shows me the real Rys. And so I march toward her, taking her into my arms.

"You seem stressed out. Can I help you with it?" I whisper in her ear, nuzzling her neck. She smells like fresh flowers, summer, and love. I can't believe I've been able to behave around her for this long. If she tells me to stop, I will, but it's going to be too fucking hard to let her go.

"Are you a therapist or a yoga instructor?" she jokes.

"I can be either one. I'll teach you some breathing techniques that I bet you've never practiced—all while you scream my name."

Before she can talk back, I kiss her soft lips. It's a slow prelude. I'm asking for permission to take the next step. Thank fuck, she kisses me back. Rys opens for me, allowing my tongue to clash with hers. I press her firmly against me. My hand runs up and down her back as I all but devour her with this kiss.

"I want you so fucking much," I groan against her mouth.

"Please," she says with a throaty voice.

I pick her up and drag her through the house, all the way up to the master bedroom where she's been staying. I'm burning with lust, ready to drive into her again and again. When I set her feet back on the floor, I stop from pouncing on her and say, "Are you sure about this? I want you so much it hurts, but I don't want you to regret it."

"We know the score, right? It's temporary."

But it's not, and how do I convince her I'm playing for keeps? I made the mistake of letting her go once, and I should've done things differently in Vegas, but I won't regret any of it.

All I have is the future and moving forward. That's the plan, to fall in love together and find our forever. This is almost like the playoffs. No, this is much more than attempting to win the Stanley Cup.

This is reaching for her heart, making it, and her, mine— surrendering my soul to her.

This is the future I never thought I wanted until I let her go.

This is the rest of our lives.

"Nothing else matters tonight, only you," I say and trail my lips along her jaw.

"We should talk," she whimpers when I begin to nibble her ear.

I pull up the t-shirt she's wearing, taking it off, and kiss her collarbone all the way to her beautiful breasts. "About how you like it? I remember. Rough at times and slow and deep too…you have an eclectic taste when it comes to sex."

"That's not—" She whimpers when I begin to push her jeans down.

"Are you wet for me, Rys?"

"Cas." The desperation in her voice makes the ache in my cock painful. I'm nearly exploding, and I haven't even started with her yet. "I need you to touch me."

I grin and set her on the bed, where I crawl over her and finish undressing her. I stare at her beautiful body. On Saturday, when she stripped for me, I wanted to slide inside her and claim her, but I knew I would regret doing something while she was under the influence. Tonight, I'm going to feast on her and try to feed the hunger I've carried for so long.

Leaning down, I capture one of her nipples with my mouth. I swirl my tongue around the tight bud while my fingers pinch the other. Her hips move up, trying to find some friction between her legs, but I ignore her. I want to tease her, make her needy.

"Please, Caspian," she begs as I continue torturing her delicious breasts.

I slide my free hand down her torso, finding her apex. My index finger finds her wet, dripping for me. I can't help but groan against her boobs, almost biting the one I'm savoring. She opens her legs wider, luring me inside her.

Instead of undressing and thrusting myself in, I push two fingers into her pussy, landing my thumb on her clit. I move my mouth to hers, fucking her with my hand, taking her to the next high, making her ready for me.

"More," she says between shallow, desperate breaths.

Each moan, word, and pant feeds my need to thrust my fingers deeper and faster.

I move lower and put my mouth on her pussy. My fingers still pushing, thrusting…making love to her. Her voice suddenly disappears, she stiffens for a second, then her mouth calls my name while her body explodes in pleasure. My body misses her as I stand up to undress and look for the condoms, tearing the wrapper and rolling it down my cock.

Climbing on the bed, I kneel in between her legs. "Rys," I whisper her name like a prayer, a last word before everything changes, the beginning of what might be a different life.

I don't say more, just sink every inch of my length inside her. I go slowly, staring at her beautiful brown eyes as I immerse into her, fusing us. This time I pray to God that we stay together like this. I kiss her hard, muffling our moans as I thrust myself inside her.

The softness of her body gives me hope. It invites me to touch heaven.

I reach the sky. I finally touch my missing star.

We're burning through the night.

Rys makes me feel whole again.

I'm finally wrapped in a bubble where only we exist.

I'm home.

Chapter Twenty-Seven

Rys

THE REST OF THE WEEK, I live in a fantasy world where only Cas and I exist. Whenever I want to discuss our situation, he uses his mouth and his body to make me forget.

On Saturday, when he suggests we take a boat ride along Lake Oswego, I thought we would be able to talk about boundaries and our future. Not together, but I need more than *we have to lie low for now.*

I didn't expect to have sex during the excursion. The only time we discuss anything important is when I tell him that as of Monday, I'm heading back to work. It's inevitable, and I dread it because what if they ask me questions? He's concerned because he'll be traveling for the next few days.

In the morning, he has me for breakfast, then we eat our actual breakfasts together and take a shower—where he dirties me up again before he washes me. I don't think temporary marriages are supposed to include this much sex, but I can't bring myself to say no. He's too persuasive and I'm addicted to his body and his big cock.

When Lincoln arrives home, I ask him to drive us up to Baker's Creek instead of the clinic. I think it's best if we talk about my circumstances. Leyla doesn't see me as a complication, but I think it might be best if she lets me go.

After the two-and-a-half-hour drive, I ask Lincoln to pull over at the coffee shop where I order a latte with extra shots and the most decadent pastry I see in their showcase—a chocolate croissant. I sit down at one of their tables and savor every bite as I slowly pack away all my thoughts of the past week, including Thad.

Earlier, he left a voicemail demanding we talk. He called me a few names and said I'd pay for betraying him. He claimed Cameron is having problems because of me—I'm the bitch in this situation.

He's wrong, and I have to push away those thoughts. There's no use lingering on a relationship that was clearly never what I thought it was. By the time I'm brushing all my crumbs up into a napkin and leaving the coffee shop, I feel much lighter.

I'm ready to see Leyla.

Lincoln is outside waiting. I point toward the animal hospital. "It's within walking distance. I'll be fine here."

He nods.

I'm determined to do as many hard things today as I can. Leyla won't be happy with what I'm going to say, but hopefully, she'll be okay with it. I don't like taking advantage of her good nature, but I could use a good portion of it today.

She's in one of the exam rooms when I slip in the back door, so I pop in to say hi to the reception area. One of the women, who I haven't met before, is visibly taken aback to see me. It tells me she knows who I am through the news cycle and not just from coworkers.

Melinda, the receptionist I do know, hangs up the phone and smiles at me before delegating her duties to the other woman and gently guiding me by the shoulders out of the reception area.

"Rys, how are you?" Melinda is everyone's work mom, and it makes me feel a little guilty about my own mother. I still haven't called her back. "I watched your wedding on TikTok. You have good taste, girl."

I wince.

"It's all good. So...you're really married? To your hockey player, right? The one you and Dan talk about all the time?"

I freeze, then force myself to nod. I think my smile might be more of a grimace than an actual smile.

"What was his name again? I'm sorry for not remembering, dear."

My shoulders drop in relief. Oh, thank God, maybe she'll never know the difference, and I won't have to fess up to meeting Cas in Vegas and getting so drunk I can barely remember the wedding. Melinda definitely doesn't need to ever hear any of that.

"Cas," I say. "His name is Cas."

"Cas," she repeats. "How cute. Is that short for anything?"

I blink at her. "For Cas—"

"Rys!" A familiar squeal saves me from absolute embarrassment. I turn gratefully to see Dan. A huge, gray pit bull is tugging him along the hallway, and when he sees my attention suddenly shift in his direction, he immediately bounces up and puts his long front legs on my hips. I laugh and pat him before gently removing his paws from me.

"Oh my God, Fisky, you know better, don't you?" Dan coos at the giant pit bull who looks back at him with doleful brown eyes that are impossible to ignore. He turns back to me. "Don't you dare leave the premises before I come back from talking to his person. We have a lot to catch up on. I. Watched. The. Videos. All of them."

Is he also talking about the video of Cam and Thad or just the wedding?

"Okay," I agree, patting Fisky one more time before he's off to the races again and dragging Dan toward the front. Melinda follows them in that direction with a wave to me, and then I'm alone in the hallway again, waiting for Leyla.

It doesn't take her too much longer to appear. When she sees me, she puts both hands on her hips and looks me over. I let myself be studied and only hang my head in shame a little bit.

"How are things with Cas?" she asks.

"Confusing," I mutter.

"That's not exactly what one says during the honeymoon period." Leyla snorts and then jerks her head toward the empty exam room. I follow inside and close the door. It won't be completely private because even behind a closed door, voices carry if you're really listening for them, but at least this way I won't have to see who does the listening.

"What's bothering you?"

I start by playing Thad's voicemail.

"Send it to Hadley or Cas's agent." She taps her chin. "Actually, send it to Pierce. He can start building a case of harassment if this continues."

"That's—"

"You need to be proactive. How about you two? Are you settling into this marriage?"

"I shouldn't. It's temporary."

She shakes her head. "I remember you talking about him as if he could hang the moon for you if you had called him back."

"He lied about who he was, and his life is different from

mine. Who wants to be with a boring veterinarian? He can have a fun woman who'll be accepted by his family."

"What do you mean?"

I tell her about my visit to Santa Cruz. She listens, and once I'm done, she says, "It sounds like they were observing you. Were they mean to you?"

"Other than the poor jokes from one of his older brothers, no. It's just—"

"If one of my brothers-in-law married a stranger in Vegas, I would be shoving her in a small room and torturing her until I figured out if she's legit. It's not that I don't like her, but I have to protect them. I'm not defending them, but I understand why they weren't rolling out the red carpet. How did your mom react?"

I shrug. "We haven't spoken. But I guess Dad will greet him with his shotgun, and Mom might pull the trigger before asking questions."

She smiles. "So you understand their behavior."

"A little. I guess this isn't what I expected when…it's so strange to be married without planning it or knowing him well."

"How is he treating you?"

"Like a queen and…" I feel as my face heats up. "Sex with him is off the charts—as it was when we first met."

"Okay, so there's room to grow and maybe hope for you two."

I understand her point, but…

"You're afraid of getting hurt?"

"Yes. People have never been too kind to me. Animals, on the other hand, they love me unconditionally."

"Give him a chance, and maybe take two weeks to get your head on straight again and honeymoon with him or whatever. Then let's reconvene."

"No, I need to go back to work unless you want me to quit?"

She gasps in horror. "You're never going to leave me. Listen, we'll cover the clinic in San Fran and just work in Portland for the time being. I'd like you to consider only going in two or three days a week. It might be good for you, but I want to ensure you're taking care of yourself."

She wants me to take two weeks off and only work three days, tops? I only take one day off. I think I would go crazy if I only went to the clinic part-time.

"I'm grateful for your offer, and I might consider taking a couple more days off, everything else… I need to busy myself or I might have a nervous breakdown."

"You don't have to tell me anything, Rys," she says. "But I hope you know that if something is wrong, I'm here and willing to listen with no judgments."

Leyla has become one of my closest friends. I wonder if Avery, her sister-in-law and my best friend, will be calling me soon. She hasn't said anything. I haven't received a text in weeks. Maybe it's for the best. She's going to solve my life, and while she's at it, she'll figure out a way to off Thad and Cameron.

"I know," I promise. "And also, it's okay if there's a little bit of judgment."

She chuckles at me. "Are you busy the rest of the day? We just got some rescue puppies in, and I've heard they're quote 'extra Code-Red cute' according to Dan."

I clap my hands together in a burst of joy. There's nothing I love more in the entire world than a puppy, and Leyla knows it.

"You know where the welcome puppy center is," she says, tilting her head toward the door. "I'll see you later."

Maybe I didn't come to get a pep talk and a reminder that I'm not alone, but I feel a lot better knowing I still have my life and I'm not losing myself in the hockey world of Caspian Spearman.

Chapter Twenty-Eight

Rys

I SPEND most of the day in Baker's Creek bathing, examining, and registering the puppies. Most of them are in good health. A couple of them need special attention though. Instead of taking them home, where Leyla has a place to foster them, she leaves them at the clinic.

Lincoln drives me back to Portland. I arrive around seven and check the freezer for one of Cas's famous frozen meals. He has a chef who comes weekly to prepare food so he can just warm it up and eat it after practice or a game. I choose chicken cordon bleu. It sounds fancy enough that I can use it as an excuse to open a bottle of wine.

When I sit to eat, my phone rings. It's Mom.

A stab of agony cuts through my insides. I've been avoiding her since the morning after the wedding. It's not that I don't want to talk to her. It's just that…okay, I have no use for her pessimism when I'm in the middle of a storm. I need to surround myself with positive people who will give me good advice.

I can already hear her telling me how I'll regret marrying a stranger in Vegas. But wasn't this what she wanted for me? For me to finally get married like Milly?

As if I invoke her, my sister calls. I slide my finger across the screen and tap the speaker button. "Hey," I greet her.

"It's been more than a week," she says.

"And yet, I haven't received a wedding present. I recall showering you with an insane amount of appliances when you finally walked down the aisle—without me."

"You can't use that anymore."

"What, the presents? I thought you said wedding presents are the least I should give you after such a big life-altering step. If you ask me, that's a pretty dramatic statement."

"No, my wedding. You just did the same thing. You eloped and didn't even invite me to be part of the wedding party." She sounds bitter, and I don't understand why we're back to discussing this, but then I remember that Milly, just like Mom, likes to hold grudges.

"At least you got to watch it from the comfort of your home," I joke, taking a forkful of chicken.

"It doesn't matter. The point is that—" She pauses for dramatic effect. "Polaris, your mother and father are driving me insane."

This doesn't surprise me. The fact that Mom is calling her often or that she's playing the martyr. I'm about to dismiss her when I finally process her words. "Wait, Dad knows?"

"The entire world knows."

I knew that, but I was hoping it wouldn't reach my father. This internet thing came to fuck everyone. I never lived in the old days of anonymity, but I'm sure if my mother or father did something like what I did, they'd be able to hide everything.

"Have I ever mentioned I hate social media?"

"No, but we have a more important issue. Your parents would like to speak to you. Call them and sort this out soon." She sighs heavily. "I can't believe I'm the adult in this situation."

"You were due. It's been twenty-seven years of being a child, and may I remind you that you have children?"

"Stop!"

I wish I could end the call. I can't even remember why we're arguing. "So, to what do I owe the pleasure of this call again?"

"Dad wants to kill Caspian. He's upset he didn't ask for your hand in marriage."

"I don't recall him asking the same from Ernest."

"Well, I was already knocked up. The least Ernie could do is marry his daughter."

"You had two children, but let's go with that version."

"Not the point. He might visit you."

My heart palpitations might indicate I'm about to go into cardiac arrest. "Dad?"

"Yep."

"Persuade him to wait." My pleading tone might do the trick. "I'm not living at home."

"Where are you?"

I almost laugh. As if I'm going to tell her. She might give the address to Dad or sell it to some seedy magazine for millions. "In a secret location, enjoying my honeymoon."

"While your husband is playing against the Rangers?"

Ugh, bitch, she got me there.

"Listen, I just need you to tell me you're okay and promise you'll call our parents. I don't have time to be you."

I grab the glass of wine and drink it all. This marriage is going to kill my liver. "What do you mean by being me?"

"You're the one who makes sure there's peace in this family. You speak on my behalf to our parents."

"Maybe it's time I stop being the middleman between everyone."

"That would be painful."

It's easy for her to say that. She's not been part of this. Mom says I need to send her more money. Dad wants us to spend Christmas with him this year. They should've used their lawyer to make changes to their custody agreement. Milly learned so well from them that I was also talking on her behalf to our parents. I still do.

"It'd be freeing."

"Sometimes, you can be so selfish."

"I'll take this conversation into consideration," I say instead of telling her that she's a brat.

It's around nine when my phone rings. It's Cas video calling me.

"Hey," I answer and almost gasp as I stare at his bare, muscled, tattooed chest.

"Like what you see?"

"Maybe?"

"I can't see much of you, Mrs. Spearman. You have on too many clothes."

"Is this a FaceTime booty call?"

He chuckles. "It could be if you want. I wouldn't mind watching you come all over your hand."

"Cas, let's not start this conversation with sex."

He pouts. "Fine, but before we hang up, I want to hear you scream my name."

I roll my eyes, feigning annoyance, but I've no doubt that I'll be undressing and pulling out a couple of the toys we bought last week before this call is over.

"How was your day, beautiful? Did you go back to work?"

I tell him about Baker's Creek, my conversation with Leyla—well, except my doubts about our temporary marriage—and the puppies.

"Next time you have to foster a puppy, just bring them home."

"To your impeccable white-rugs-luxurious-couches-brand-new house?"

"Our house."

"You'd let me bring dogs into *your* home?" I repeat, ignoring the *our house* part.

"It's your place too, of course I would."

"Have you ever had a dog?"

"No."

"The D stands for destructors."

He laughs. "It's okay if they chew the entire house. Material things are replaceable. They need a home where they can feel safe and loved. You'll bring them so we can be their temporary parents, okay?"

And I melt with those words. "Okay, I'll keep that in mind."

"What else happened?"

I sigh because I have to tell him about Thad, and I do. He growls. "Send the voicemail to Lang, please. He'll take care of it. What I don't understand is why you dated the douchebag in the first place."

"I felt lonely. Dating seems to be the next step to ticking all the boxes in the game of life. He was there, and he seemed nice."

"Nice? You dated him because he's nice?"

"He wasn't that bad. The last few weeks we were together he was making a real effort, you know. I guess he thought things were over with Cameron."

Those eyes darken when he asks, "Were you falling for him?"

"I was trying to believe that something was going to happen, but we weren't compatible," I say, not ending the sentence with *unlike you and me.*

"Sounds like you were forcing it," he states.

"Probably. I don't want to make a big deal out of this. Releasing the video was enough."

The way he looks at me makes me miss him. "Why don't you hop on a plane and come with me? I need you."

I try to lighten the mood by asking, "You want your own puck bunny?"

He laughs. "If you want to play that scenario, we can do it. You'll pretend to break into my room, wait for me naked, and I'll fuck you all night."

"Has that ever happened?"

Cas flinches. "A few times when I was a rookie."

"How about now?"

He shakes his head. "My agent makes sure my room is booked under a pseudonym, so no one bothers me. I stopped doing stupid things long ago, and as I mentioned before, after you, I've had no interest in being with anyone."

"Why?"

"Because after that night, I had the feeling that I belonged to you."

"Cas, we…" I have no idea how to finish that sentence. *Don't leave me, let me go, let's rewind time and ignore each other in Vegas.*

But I don't want any of that. I want him. Is that even possible?

"We can talk about that later. Why don't you show me what's under my shirt? I bet those tits are needy and ready for my mouth."

I squirm, and for the rest of the call, I just follow his orders and touch myself until I come hard and loud.

One week and he'll be back home.

Chapter Twenty-Nine

Caspian

A WEEK.

It's been one week since the last time I saw Rys.

Last night I arrived home at midnight. She was sleeping, and I didn't want to bother her. I slept in the guest room and left the house before six in the morning. I had to run some drills. I did leave a note next to the coffee maker and sent her flowers to the clinic. I used the concierge company Lang recommended so no one can trace Rys to me.

I just hope she comes to our after-game celebrations.

The bar the team frequents is uptown from the arena, just far enough that the fans aren't likely to be there after a game and close enough to not kill the vibe. Tonight's game against the Canucks was one of our best in weeks and our first game back on home ice since the break, so drinks are pretty much a given.

Rys texts me, confirming Shelly is picking her up and they're coming together, which is a relief. The guys have been in good humor about the whole situation, but it will help considerably to calm the waters if Rys puts in a few appearances.

Some of them are concerned that she's a gold-digging puck bunny who just flits from one player to another until she caught one in a marriage, which is so far from the truth it's almost laughable.

I understand where they're coming from—protective of me even when I already have several older brothers for that—but I'm confident once they meet Rys, they'll be a lot less concerned.

When she arrives, my jaw drops. She looks hot as hell. She glances around before finally spotting me at the bar where I ordered her favorite vodka seltzer. She smiles and makes her way over to me. I take her into my arms and kiss her hard. When I finish, she looks at me flustered.

"Good game," she says as she sidles up next to me.

"Did you actually watch it?" I ask her, amused, wrapping an arm around her waist and kissing her forehead.

"You don't have to do this," she whispers.

"What?"

"Pretend with so much PDA."

But wanting to touch and kiss Rys all the time is as natural as breathing to me. I guess I have to change my tactics because she thinks I'm in this just for the PR and not because I want to be with her. Do I think this fire between us will extinguish? No, it won't. Every time we're together the flame gets bigger.

It's been almost three years since I met her, and she's always been on my mind. Now that she's here, I'll brand my soul into hers and carve her name in my heart.

"Who says I'm pretending, babe?"

"Cas?"

I don't understand if she's asking a question, gasping my name because she wants me the same way I want her, or warning me…her tone is too confusing.

"Yes?"

"Please behave. I'm uncomfortable with PDA. More so when people are watching me."

I pay attention to the room and notice that everyone —*everyone*—is gawking at us.

Giving her an apologetic smile, I say, "Sorry. I can't keep my hands away from my strikingly hot wife. So, you were saying you watched the game."

"I had it on while talking to Milly," she reports. "Shelly came over during the third so we could make it over here if you guys won."

"I'm glad she's including you," I say honestly.

"She's nice," Rys says. "She's been really helpful."

"Have you met any of the other wives yet? I'm sure a lot of them will be here tonight."

Her face twists into a frown, but she just buries it in my bicep. The bartender arrives with her drink while she's still hiding, so I run a hand through her hair and lean down to ask her teasingly, "Will vodka help?"

This does the trick, and she emerges with eager, grabby hands for the glass. She only takes a short sip when she brings it to her mouth, the color on her lips transferring in a perfect imprint on the rim. I want to kiss her badly, but instead, I squeeze her hip.

"Can I introduce you around?" I ask.

She nods, both hands holding her drink in front of her like a protection amulet. I guide her over to where Spacey is holding down a table with Shelly and a few younger guys who tend to follow him around like ducklings. Shelly slides a supportive smile at Rys as we come over, and Rys seems to stand a little straighter beside me.

Chapter Thirty

Rys

MARRIED LIFE IS a lot different from an episode of *I Love Lucy*.

I don't love that I have a credit card, a joint bank account, and access to Cas's schedule. It makes things...not temporary. We don't speak much about our relationship, but that doesn't mean we ignore each other. We talk about his family, mine, work, and sometimes we just read in silence before heading to bed.

It's Tuesday after a game when my phone rings. I'm hoping

it's Cas, but instead Avery's name appears on the screen. When I slide my finger across the screen to answer, she says, "Tell me again you're not doing this under duress. Or wait, blink twice right now if you need help."

I give her a wide-eyed look that I hope communicates how done I am with this conversation. "I'm fine. This is my choice."

"Yeah, but, Rys, honey, is it a good one?" she asks. "I already asked Ben to go and kick Caspian's ass. He said he can't. He fears he might lose a finger or two. It's not good for a surgeon to be missing digits or limbs."

I wish she were near so I could throw one of the nearby couch pillows at her head. I notice she's sipping wine. "How's life?"

"We're not talking about me. I'm concerned for you. My sisters-in-law aren't telling me anything. Something about confidentiality. My brother, Mills, keeps ignoring my calls and sending me vague texts," she complains.

"You could've called me."

"I did, right after I found out about your nuptials and tried to reach the family."

"So you found out today? Where were you?"

She glances everywhere but at the camera.

"Avery?"

"It's not important. Focus on what matters, okay? Rearranging your entire life around a man is not going to work, not for an independent woman like you."

I roll my eyes at her and march toward the laundry room. I might as well start folding clothes if I'm going to entertain her nonsense.

"It's not my entire life that's changing," I say. "Even if I made a few changes, it'd be because we're married. Married people do this sort of thing."

"Tell me what happened. How did you end up with him?"

I should write a tell-all just for friends and family. Maybe a podcast or something I can just hand out or replay because it's exhausting to recount the worst weekend of my life.

"You don't have to stay married though," Avery grumbles at me. "I thought you were trying to make things work with what's his face, and now you're married—not dating—*married* to his archenemy. You barely even know the guy. You slept with him like three years ago, and then you run into him at a casino fresh off finding your actual boyfriend fucking someone else, and now you're married? You cannot tell me the sex was that good."

"The sex is even better," I say. It's true, and I know it will annoy her. She scowls at me.

"Good sex does not make a marriage."

I take a deep breath and fill the basket with the warm clothing from the dryer before heading to my room to fold it.

"Rys, don't avoid me."

"We're trying to make this less of a PR disaster for him, so we're going to be married for a while, okay?"

"I just don't want to see you getting hurt when this inevitably falls apart," she says.

"If I already know it will end one day, what's there to get hurt about? It's basically a friends-with-benefits thing until then. It'll be fine."

I try my best to sound cool and calm about it, even as my words ignite a small flame of doubt in me. When has friends with benefits ever actually been a good idea for anyone? I just hope I won't catch feelings like they're the common cold—or I might die.

Avery looks like she's thinking the same thing, but instead of continuing the fight, she takes a sip of her wine and puckers her lips.

"Fine," she says after a few more sips. "Suit yourself. But I get to say *I told you so* when this makes you cry later."

I sigh.

"Fair's fair," I agree. I set the basket on the bed and pull out a shirt.

"What are you doing?"

"Folding clothes," I say, setting the phone on the nightstand.

"We should go to Paris on a shopping spree."

"Sorry, my wallet is thinking downtown Portland."

She laughs. "You should make your husband pay for the trip."

"It's not like that."

"Then how is it? I need to know more. Relationships fascinate me."

"Ask Ben to teach you."

She gives me a wicked smile. "I might ask for a little friends-with-benefits treatment. What can go wrong?"

I don't tell her that having sex with a friend is completely different from what I'm referring to, but she won't listen. I adore Avery, but sometimes she's a little too detached from reality.

Mom calls right after Avery hangs up... I can no longer avoid answering. I've dodged her so far, but there's only so long I can do it before she shows up on my doorstep. I swipe to answer the call reluctantly.

"Well," she huffs as soon as I've said hello. "It's nice to know you're alive."

I roll my eyes at the ceiling and lie on the couch. I can sense I'm in for an earful, and I've let her build up a full head of steam about it.

"What do you have to say for yourself?" she demands.

"Not much that you probably don't already know," I admit. "I got married. Everything's fine."

"Married!" she practically shrieks. "After everything I've taught you. After how you were raised. Why would you ever even think of getting married to a stranger? You know it will never last."

Is it possible to build a long-lasting marriage out of nothing more than a drunken mistake just to spite my mother? Probably not, and besides, that's not what Cas wants anyway. This marriage will fall apart in a few months, but until then, at least it can make my mom uncomfortable.

"I love him, Mom," I say with a very fake pout. "Why wouldn't I marry him?"

"Men like that do not stay married, and you know it."

My mother thought all men were "men like that." It had been the theme of my sister's and my education growing up. It's impressive either one of us turned out somewhat normal when it comes to romantic relationships.

"I don't know what you mean," I say, even though I do. "Cas isn't like that."

And the thing is, even if she'll never believe me, I actually do think that part's true. Cas isn't like that. He would never do what Thad did to me—I know that with bone-deep certainty. In fact, despite this whole Vegas-marriage circus, he seems like the type of guy to get married once and stick with it for life. It's a shame I fucked that up for him.

"All men are like that," my mother says in the exact tone of voice I'd imagined her saying that phrase a few minutes ago. I nearly allow my snort of laughter to escape me but just barely keep it in while I muffle the phone. "Every last damn one."

"Did you need something, Mom?" I prompt her, hoping we can maybe cut this short. It's been a long day of decisions, and I only have a teaspoon of patience left for this. "Otherwise, I need to go make myself dinner."

It takes another half hour to get her off the phone, but while talking, I decide to just order delivery instead of dealing with the random assortment of frozen meals and dry goods in the kitchen. I've never been more thankful when the doorbell rings.

Chapter Thirty-One

Caspian

"OKAY, so here's what's going to happen." Hadley claps her hands together as she looks Rys and me over. "First, we'll get a few shots of Rys and you skating together, then we're going to sit you down and play a little game—kind of like *The Newlywed Game*, that old TV show? Just some light trivia about each other."

It's around ten in the morning and I'm freshly released from one of the assistants who had been making my post-morning-skate-shower hair look good. Rys doesn't get mobbed by any assistants because she arrives looking perfectly camera-ready.

She'd been surprisingly chill when agreeing to this, but I can see she's nervous now that she's here. I'm not sure if taking her hand would be welcomed or not, so I just hover nearby. She reminds me of my younger brother Heath. Last night she was studying all the answers for the trivia. Like Heath, she asked me to quiz her until she got every answer right.

I… I decided not to study, and as a reward for knowing all the basics about my career and the little people know about my private life, we had mind-blowing sex. No one should say I'm not a thoughtful husband. I know how to distract my wife.

"If there's anything you're uncomfortable with at any point, let me know," Hadley says to Rys, her eyes serious and sharp. "It's my job to make you look good, and happy people always look good."

It's a line I've heard before, and I smile at Hadley over Rys's shoulder in thanks. I know she's going above and beyond for us here, and I'm not sure what I've done to deserve it. I'm one of the worst interviewees on the Orcas, but I guess years of not actually complaining about taking an intermission interview have added up in karma points.

She leaves me alone with Rys for a moment while she runs off to grab a pair of skates for Rys.

"You ever skated before?" I ask.

"Um…" She trails off. Her eyes have gone a little squinty as she thinks about it. "I'm positive I have. Am I positive when I last skated? Absolutely not."

"I'll keep you upright," I promise her.

"You'd better," she says. "If my butt touches the ice, you're in so much trouble, mister."

I click my tongue at her and push her toward the tunnel where Hadley has just re-emerged with a pair of skates, a t-shirt, and thick socks she must have snagged directly out of the gift shop based on the huge Orcas logo on them. Rys takes them in good humor, holding up the t-shirt to reveal a shirsey with my name and number on the back. And damn, I hadn't even thought of what it would do to me to see her wearing my number. Suddenly this whole situation just got a lot hotter for me.

Rys ducks into one of the athletic trainers' small offices to quickly change, and when she comes out, Hadley reaches to knot the t-shirt in the back, pulling it tighter against Rys's breasts. I can't help but let my eyes linger.

"Stop looking at me like that," Rys hisses at me as soon as Hadley, apparently satisfied with the wardrobe change, walks back over to the small crew.

"Like what?" I smirk as she huffs her way over to the bench to start pulling on the socks and skates.

"You know exactly what." She waves one of the socks at me threateningly.

I laugh and get down on one knee before pulling up her right foot and helping her wiggle it inside. I tighten the laces with a lifetime of ease and then move on to the other skate. She's ready to go in minutes. I sit down next to her and pull out my own skates from the gear bag I'd dragged out here earlier.

"Is this going to make my feet hurt?" she asks, frowning down at her skates.

"Probably," I say cheerfully, standing up from the bench. "But if they do, I promise to kiss them better later."

She takes my extended hand with a grumble and wobbles unsteadily next to me as I walk her to the boards. Hadley and the crew are all set up with some mats out on one side of the ice and some empty space at the other end for us to skate.

"You want us to just skate?" I holler over to her.

Hadley throws me a thumbs-up and says something to one of the camera guys, who also gives me a thumbs-up a moment later after checking his viewfinder. I turn back to Rys.

"You ready?" I ask her. I open the boards and step onto the ice, anchoring myself before offering her my hands again. She takes them, looking more skeptical by the moment, but still gingerly stepping onto the ice. "Easy does it."

Her legs splay apart almost immediately, but it's easy enough to keep her upright as we grip each other's wrists. It only takes her a lap or two before she lets me skate beside her instead of in front of her, still wobbling, but upright enough to at least be comfortable clinging to the boards instead of just me.

"Just a few more spins around, and we've got it," the camera guy calls out.

"Hold her hand!" Hadley adds.

I laugh and turn to Rys, very theatrically offering my hand to her. She takes it with a mock bow, and I swing our joined hands between us as she still holds on to the boards with her other hand.

"You want to go fast one time before we're done?" I ask.

"How fast?"

"I'll make sure you don't fall or hit the boards."

"Ugh, fine." She gives me both of her hands again, and I start skating backward.

As soon as I have some more maneuverability, I take off, pushing her forward and then turning us so I have my back to the boards. We hurtle across the ice, and she shrieks, but holds on tight until I pull us to a stop and let her tiny frame run into me so I can pull her into a hug. I laugh as I pull her off the ice for a second.

"Oh my God, Cas, that was way too fast," she says, and it's so quiet in my ear that I hope it's just for me, and no mics picked it up. I love the way she says my name. I think if I could, I would make it so no one else could ever hear her say it.

I put her back down and gently push her toward the other end of the ice. We take a few minutes to take off our skates and put our shoes back on before we're put in two high director's chairs that are right in front of the home goal. We get through our trivia game with a decent showing and lots of giggles from Rys when I pull faces at her while the camera's on her and not me.

"It's going to be really cute, you guys," Hadley promises as we wrap up. "It'll probably be out tomorrow or the next day, and we'll show it up on the Jumbotron."

"On the Jumbotron?" Rys's eyes bulge so big I think they might pop out. "I thought it was just for like...social media."

Hadley laughs. "It's for both. We have to fill all those commercial breaks and intermissions with something. Besides, a lot more people follow us on social media than could ever fit in the arena."

"Getting stage fright now?" I tease Rys.

"No, just..." She casts her eyes around the empty stands of our much smaller practice facility. "It's a lot of people."

"It'll be good," Hadley promises.

"Okay, yeah." Rys nods her head as if she's still convincing herself. This time I take her hand and slide our fingers together with a squeeze. She squeezes back hard and keeps our hands intertwined. "You keep promising that, but every time, I feel dragged deeper into a rabbit hole."

"As long as we're together, it'll be fine," I promise.

Not sure what I just pledged, but I'll make sure that she doesn't get hurt.

Not at all.

Chapter Thirty-Two

Rys

OBVIOUSLY, when dating Thad, I'd gotten used to the rhythm of him going on road trips constantly, but somehow with Cas, it's different.

Maybe it's because I'm actually in Cas's house and we speak to each other daily, seeing how empty it is while he's gone, whereas my relationship with Thad had been long-distance more than not.

Not being with Cas is a little spooky. The entire house has large glass windows everywhere, and even though I know no one can see in at night, it's still a little disconcerting. We're surrounded by woods up here, making it feel more isolated than it actually is. In reality, we're only a short ride away from the city center, but it feels like I'm in the middle of nowhere, alone.

Maybe the night's loneliness is what pushes me to volunteer to take two puppies that need a home. It was only going to be a small Maltese mix. But then there's this pup with beautiful, huge, brown eyes that convinced me to take him home too. I'm only human, after all. No one can resist a Newfoud-wolfhound puppy pout. No one.

I'm thankful Leyla listened to me and set up a pet store next to the animal clinic. Before I place them in my car, I buy everything they need and order a couple of kennels for them. Training them to sleep in their kennels while we wait for someone to adopt them will be good.

We spend the first night in the living room. The following day, Lincoln has a couple of kennels in the SUV.

"You didn't have to do that," I say.

"Yesterday, you refused to put them in the trunk. I thought it might be easier to convince you if they have a safe place where I can transport them. How long are you keeping them?"

As I put the little girl in her kennel, I answer, "Not sure. They're too cute. I bet someone will adopt them as soon as we post their pictures on the website."

"When is that going to happen?"

I tap my chin. "I'm guessing she's about five weeks old and he… I have to do the medical examination today. He might be eight weeks old and—"

"You like him?"

"Yeah, but I doubt Caspian wants to have them as guests for long," I confess. Saying the words out loud reminds me we didn't talk last night. He didn't even text me to wish me a good night.

It's okay though. We're not together and what we have is

casual. However, repeating that doesn't do the trick. I miss him, and I'm a little hurt.

When we get to the office, Leyla is there looking at some charts.

"If I knew you'd be here, I would've come earlier," I say, heading to the office.

"I heard you took a couple of puppies."

"Like one does when they need a foster home," I answer, setting them in the dog beds I bought yesterday.

"What are you calling them?" she asks me as she picks up the little Maltese princess and cuddles her.

One perk of being a veterinarian is that bringing your dogs or foster animals to work is no big deal.

"For now, he's 'big boy' or 'precious boy,' and she's 'princess' or 'little one,'" I admit. I make a kissy noise at the big boy, and his head flops in my direction. He's so cute I wanna cry.

"Big boy needs a big name," Leyla says in a baby voice. She sits down in one of the rolling office chairs while cuddling with the princess. "Are you leaving them here tonight?"

"No," I say quickly. "They'll be with me until we find a good family for them."

"Your husband okay with that?" she teases. She's been enjoying referring to Cas by only "your husband" even though I know she knows his name. I think she likes to see me squirm every time she says it.

"I don't need his permission to bring a dog home," I shoot back. Which is true. I mean, he told me the last time I could bring them, and he wouldn't care. Plus, Cas is too cute to be objectionable.

"I'm thinking Leonidas or Apollo or something appropriately fierce and warrior-like." Leyla swerves back to the topic of names.

"Too easy," I say, discarding them immediately.

"What was his intake name?" she asks, looking up from where she's grabbed both of his front paws in a shake.

I scrunch my nose up.

"Spork?"

"Like the *Star Trek* guy?" she asks.

"No, that's Spock. Spork like…spoon-fork? I don't know."

"Oh, big boy, you definitely need a better name than that, don't you? And you, little one, should be Camilla or Annie." She returns to her baby voice and kisses the puppy's nose. The puppy looks nonplussed about the entire situation and blinks sleepily at us.

"I might not name them since they'll be leaving soon," I almost pout.

She snorts. "I doubt they'll leave your house."

"How can you say that?"

"You're fostering two—they're going to bond like brother and sister, which will be super cute. When it comes to adoption, it's going to be tough to place them together and you won't want to split them."

I huff. "You're wrong."

"Uh-huh. If you're right, I'll give you fifty dollars. I should get going," she says, setting the little one next to the big pup. "I came to Portland with Pierce. He needed to check on a client. We have a day date."

"Where are the kids?"

She grins. "Uncle Beacon and Aunt Grace came home yesterday. They offered to babysit. Let me know how things go when Cas gets home." Leyla sighs dramatically and pouts first at me and then at the puppy. "Good luck with your new children. I'll see you when it's time to do the official paperwork."

I roll my eyes at her.

"I put fifty dollars on her keeping the dogs," Leyla says loudly, to no one in particular.

Is there some kind of office pool going on? I don't even ask.

"They are just fosters," I insist.

"Foster fail in the making," Leyla claims. "That's what happened with my dogs. I tried to get this hot guy to adopt Buster—I knew they were perfect for each other."

"What went wrong?"

She smiles. "I ended up adopting both, Buster and Pierce."

I burst into laughter. "I had no idea."

"That's how we met, he brought him to the animal hospital I was interning for, and one thing led to another."

"Well, that's not going to happen to us."

She pats my arm. "Sure. Let's go with that."

Everyone in the hospital volunteers to watch the puppies while I'm doing consultations. The day is long, but thankfully, I arrive home a little before seven. I find the boxes of everything I ordered online the previous day. I have plenty of time to get everything set up in the house for the puppies, including some child gates and toys to keep them contained and occupied.

Cas would be home sometime tonight. I still haven't heard from him, but I don't think much of it. There has to be a good reason why he hasn't called me. I don't think this is over yet, is it?

Princess and Big Boy look at me, and I don't know if they're worried, or they just need to go out to the backyard. I do the latter and ignore the worry cemented in the pit of my stomach.

Chapter Thirty-Three

Caspian

As I DRIVE HOME, I feel the tightness on my shoulders disappear. Yesterday was stressful as fuck. Dawn Spearman, better known by my siblings as the mother, finally caught up to me. I've been avoiding her calls and texts since the Vegas wedding. I'm ashamed to admit I blocked her number.

If I have to choose between her and Rys, well, Lysander told me to choose Rys. I don't understand why, but he told me to be extra careful. He might not be thrilled about my marriage, but he understands Rys matters to me—a lot.

Last night, when the game ended, my mom was in the locker room. Talk about embarrassing and shameful moments. I'm the captain of the team and my mother is waiting for me. Thankfully, the coach ushered us to a private office where she gave me an earful. I had to take her to dinner.

Knowing Helicopter Dawn, I took drastic measures and erased Rys's information from my phone and all our texts. Even her pictures. I adore my mother, but she is worse than a CIA agent. I don't know if she tried to snoop in my things, but it's better to be safe than having Mom nag my wife.

Of course, my mother wanted to know more about Rys, and during dinner, she interrogated me. I didn't answer much. Though, the conversation made me wonder what was going on between her and Fern because she blamed her for what's happening to the family.

I have no fucking idea if there is something going on, and no one has told me.

Other than the headache after our dinner, I didn't say good night to Rys or talk to her at all. I could've called my agent, Mills, or Leyla to get her information, but I didn't want to explain myself. It's already too fucking awkward to have my mother in the locker room.

When I arrive home, the lights in my living room are still on. I sigh with relief, knowing that Rys is both home and still awake. She's in the kitchen waiting for the microwave when I walk in from the garage. She smiles brightly at me, her whole face lighting up, and it makes my stomach flip.

I greet her with a lingering kiss and an arm around her waist. When she pulls back, she's still smiling. "You're home."

"Thank fuck," I say, kissing her again. "I missed you too much. Sorry for not calling. I have a little tale for you."

"Okay, but before that, I have a surprise," she says, bouncing on her toes.

"A surprise?" I ask. "Is it red and lacy?"

She taps me on the nose with one finger and shakes her head.

"Nope," she says. "Much cuter."

"Much...cuter?" I ask, confused. I don't care about cute, more like hot and lacy and... I need sex.

"Close your eyes."

I comply, letting myself be herded toward the living room. There's a smell in the room I can't quite place, but Rys seems excited, so I go forward without asking questions.

"Okay, so don't panic when you open your eyes," she says.

"Did you sell all my furniture or something?" That's all I can guess. "Why would I be panicking?"

"Open your eyes on three. Two. One!"

It takes a moment to realize what I'm seeing—there is a small playpen set up in the middle of my living room where my couch would usually be, but it has been shoved to the wall. In the playpen, there is a large brown pile of fur I almost mistake for a pillow at first until I see two large brown eyes staring dolefully back at me. Next to it hides a white fluff ball, which I assume is a toy.

"Where did you get a dog?" I ask and then immediately realize what a stupid question it is. She works at an animal hospital. It's pretty obvious where she got the dog. "No, wait, don't answer that, dumb question. How about why do you have a dog in our house? Are we fostering?"

"There are two of them," she says.

I walk closer and realize the little fluff ball next to the big pillow is also a puppy. I bend and pick the pup up. "Well, hello there, I almost missed you."

"They needed a foster, and I was right there, and they're so cute..." Rys says. "She's only five weeks, and we think he's about eight weeks old, even though he looks like a full-grown puppy. Usually, Newfound-wolfhound are big boys, mixed with an Irish wolfhound they are...well, you can see his size. But not to worry, they're just fosters though."

"What's your name, cutie?" I ask the little girl that fits perfectly in my hands. She's so tiny.

"If you really hate the idea of keeping them around, I can take them back tomorrow, but I was hoping you would give them a chance because, otherwise, they might have to live in one of the offices at work."

"You're telling me the puppies that are so cute you couldn't resist would just languish in an office at work, and no one else would try to take them home?"

She pouts at me. "Well, maybe they would, but then I wouldn't get to take them home for a few days."

"I'm starting to understand now," I say. "You had to take the puppies home so no one else would."

"Exactly," she says.

"And how long will the puppies be staying with us?" I ask.

"Um, it depends. A few weeks tops. Once they're ready to be adopted."

I laugh at her and then pull her close by the waist, so my lips are against her ear.

"And what do I get for accommodating not one, but two puppies for a couple of weeks?" I ask.

She purses her lips in thought for a moment and turns in my arms.

"For starters, you can have naming rights," she says. "The rest is still up for negotiation, but I drive a hard bargain."

"Oh, do I need to call my agent?"

She plays with the top button on my shirt and flicks it open.

"I don't think that will be necessary," she says and pulls me in for a kiss.

"So, your mom kidnapped you, and you had to delete all the information on your phone?"

"Just yours," I correct her.

"Why?"

"Dawn is nosy. She wants to meet you, and I can't let that happen yet," I explain as I get ready for bed.

"Mia and Ralph are judging you."

I laugh. "They're downstairs sound asleep."

"We should be with them," Rys says, kissing my jaw. "Next time you don't call, maybe I should be the one doing the virtual booty call."

"Please do. Also, text me your information and any pictures you have of us together."

"All of them?"

I'm about to tell her to put them on the cloud when my phone rings. I usually wouldn't answer, but it's Heath.

"What's up, doc?" I answer, heading to the closet to pull a pair of boxers from the drawers.

"Dawn Spearman, or as you like to call her, Helicopter Dawn." He lets out a loud breath. "She came to the ER."

My heart stops. "Is she okay?"

"Depending on what you define as okay? I think she needs therapy and to stop manipulating her children with her health."

"What do you mean?"

"She made up some shit about having heart palpitations and was breathing erratically in the middle of the emergency room. Obviously, she was admitted. I was paged, and when I arrived at the room, she began to interrogate me about your wife."

"What the fuck?"

"My thoughts exactly. I just came home and texted Lysander. He's on his way to the roof. I bet Aslan and Gatsby will join us. This is just too screwed up, you know?"

"I couldn't agree more." I sigh and tell him what happened yesterday. "But why go through the trouble of getting admitted?"

"She couldn't get much out of you, and therefore, she tried me. I didn't answer her calls and she ended up in the emergency room faking a heart attack."

"Sounds like something Dawn would do, but why?"

"I have my theories."

After a few seconds, I ask, "Are you going to share?"

"Not yet. Though, I'm just beginning to wonder if everything we lived through when we were teenagers was just a sham."

"She was catatonic."

"There's more to it than that."

"What do you want me to do?"

"Keep your wife away from her. Remember what happened with Atzi—and she's just a friend."

Sure, Atzi is *just* a friend. She and Heath have been friends for a long time. We don't know why once Mom was out of the catatonia she tried to push her out of Heath's life. We don't understand why she was so vicious with Atzi, but we're thankful the girl stuck around. I'm not sure what the doc would do without his best friend.

The same I would do without my wife?

Are we in that place yet? Is Rys that important to me?

I recall the night I went with Gatsby to get a tattoo and we both chose constellations. I can't remember what he got but it's in honor of Maia. Me, I got Ursa Minor because I wanted to remember Rys, keep a part of her.

Maybe I was branded by her soul from the moment we kissed and I just didn't understand it back then.

Now more than ever I'll keep Helicopter Dawn away from her.

"Thank you for the heads-up. Call if you guys come up with something that might help Mom. I'm concerned about her."

"Will do. How's life with Rys?"

I glance toward the bed and realize she's gone. "Interesting. I have to send you some pictures. You might be an uncle again."

"What the fuck, Cas?"

I end the call and send a picture of Mia and Ralph through the website my cousin Jackson set up a few years back. The caption reads, *Meet the new members of our family.*

I'm not surprised that it was followed by several messages.

Alex: WTF, Cas, did you seriously get married? Call me as soon as possible!

Jackson: My parents are concerned, call them.

I'm not surprised by my oldest cousins' reactions. Uncle James was close to Dad, and when he died, he and Aunt Ari helped us a lot. Their children are like older siblings, and from the sound of their texts, they want to know more about my wife and the marriage.

One day soon, I'll introduce them to Rys, and hopefully, they'll welcome her to our family.

June: Fern says your bride is adorable. I want to meet her and the pups too.

Jannette: We need an introduction ASAP, bring her to Hawaii. The honeymoon is on the house.

Jason: Congrats, Cas. Let us know when you're ready to celebrate with the family.

Aslan: Don't encourage him.

Heath: You're an asshole, Cas, but the furry niece and nephew are pretty cute.

Once I see Heath's comment, I head downstairs. Rys is hugging Ralph, and I take a picture of the two of them. If I'm lucky, this is going to be permanent. I just need to be smart about it.

Chapter Thirty-Four

Rys

WE MIGHT BE super careful with social media and our private life, but still, news spreads fast. Hadley gets wind about Mia and Ralph and texts me. She wants me to start taking pictures of the kids with Cas so he can post them on his social media.

Though she doesn't want me to open my account, she suggests I start a new one for the pups. She promises to help me manage it as long as I send her daily pictures of them.

The first time I post, I'm not sure how to feel about it, but by day four it's easy to come up with captions and even more when I can tag Cas, who reposts from the pups' account. Every morning, Lincoln picks us up from home and takes us to work. The evening is just the same, except for today when he dropped me at the arena and he went home with precise instructions on how to feed the puppies, walk them, and get them to bed.

Being at the arena during game day isn't my idea of having a good time, but I have to do it for Cas. The only reason I'm at all prepared for seeing myself on the Jumbotron is that Hadley sent me the rough cut of the video Cas and I made a few days ago.

It was cute on my phone screen, but it is beyond mortifying in real life at the arena while tens of thousands of people watch it during the first intermission. The worst part is I'm there, like physically in the arena, when it plays, and I'm warned ahead of time there will be cameras on me almost the whole night, waiting to catch my reactions.

I feel like I'm vibrating in my seat and everyone is staring at me even though I know I'm just another face in the crowd to most people. I could walk by them in the crowded concessions hall and only a few heads would turn. This is the first Orcas game I've attended in person and Cas got me a ticket up in a box so I wouldn't be in the middle of the crowd. I don't think I could've handled being up against the glass tonight.

The game itself isn't going well. The Orcas are down by two going into the second and are starting the period off on the penalty kill. Even with my still beginner-level hockey knowledge, I know they're playing sloppy tonight.

They must be tired after being on the road for so long and only having one day to rest. I had seen glimpses of this packed schedule while dating Thad, but I don't think I realized the full extent of how exhausting it was until just now. I'm starting to understand why professional hockey players need to bulk up so much during the summer months—they hardly have time to breathe during the season, and they're working so hard that it just falls off.

"Cute spot," Shelly says when I see her after the game. "You guys were adorable."

"All thanks to Hadley," I say truthfully. "She was the master-mind behind it all. I just showed up."

Shelly laughs and squeezes my arm.

"Well, regardless, I think you're adjusting well," she says. "Plus, the crowd really loved it."

I hadn't expected to find friendship with anyone in Cas's orbit, which makes Shelly's easy acceptance of me that much sweeter. I can tell her husband really loves Cas, which is good because I know that professional sports teams are not always as happy as they look.

Thad spoke a lot about his ongoing personality conflicts with some of his teammates. Most of the guys look at Cas with something close to adoration. When he comes out of the locker room, he's fresh from a shower with a towel around his neck. He smiles softly when he sees me, but a teammate calls for him from down the hall, roping him into another conversation. He gives me an apologetic look before turning back in the direction he'd come from.

"A captain never rests," Shelly says wryly beside me.

"It's nice," I say. "That they like him so much."

Shelly presses her lips together in a smile and nods.

"It is," she agrees. "He's a better captain than most I've seen —they're not always much more than franchise-chosen faces. Cas takes the job more seriously than that."

A silly part of me that feels ridiculously like a thirteen-year-old, giddy with a crush wants to sneak a picture of Cas talking seriously with two teammates, his arms crossed and eyes intense. I want to send it to Avery and moon over the guy.

I shake my head at my own thoughts. It's stupid on so many levels to allow any of these feelings to linger. This is temporary, and I have to remember that. Cas isn't mine, at least not for much longer.

Chapter Thirty-Five

Rys

Never let it be said that bathing a puppy is easy, but cleaning a Newfoud-wolfhound puppy might be one of my toughest jobs yet.

While Mia is the sweetest, most quiet puppy in the world, Ralph is a demon. So far, he's eaten a pair of Cas's favorite athletic shoes and his lucky socks—I had to mend them because he refused to put them in the trash.

I think the worst part of everything is that poor Ralph grows every day and is completely unaware of his size. He believes he's just as tiny as Mia, so he knocks into just about everything in the house and yard, which means he's often covered in dirt by the end of the day.

Today, he's decided to also take a good long soak in a water puddle in the yard, so he's dripping with mud when I call him inside. I stop him at the screen door before he can bring any of the mud inside and muck up Cas's nearly pristine white carpet.

I grab him by the collar and call for Cas behind me. This will be a two-person job, so it's good that today is a maintenance day for him. He looks sleepy when he emerges from the bedroom, but he doesn't need to be asked to put on his sandals and come outside to help me.

He takes up station at the hose and the patio, which has become the de facto dog-washing station now.

"Where is Mia?" he asks.

"In the playpen like a good puppy," I answer.

He laughs. "She's a princess. Unlike her brother who likes to play rough, don't you, Ralphie?"

"Ruff!"

"Hope you're not opposed to showering after this because I think it's gonna get messy," I say as I maneuver the squirmy puppy closer to the hose.

Ralph shakes himself vigorously just to prove my point, splattering us both with mud. I wipe it off my face as Cas laughs. He doesn't bother with the flecks that land on him and instead reaches to turn on the hose. He keeps the pressure gentle as he begins to pour it over Ralph's head. Ralph, enthused at the addition of more water, twists upward to try to bite at the water.

It takes us the better part of an hour to get him fully clean. When I finally declare him done, Cas playfully sprays me with the hose. I grab it from him and turn the spray on him, soaking him generously. His white t-shirt clings to his abs in a way that is absolutely unreal. I can't help but ogle him.

Of course, he notices and grins at me as he starts stripping right there on the patio.

"Like what you see?" he teases.

If I was a stronger woman, I would be able to resist the obvious bait, but to hell with it. I raise both my eyebrows at him and motion for him to keep going. He laughs and obliges, throwing his wet clothes to the ground and then turning and walking inside, completely naked. It's an absolute pleasure to watch him go.

"I'll be in the shower if you want to join," he calls over his shoulder. Conceited jerk. He absolutely knows what he looks like. Every part of his body is sculpted with muscles and dripping wet.

I put Ralph in the second playpen, so he doesn't disturb Mia, and quickly make my way to the master bathroom where Cas is already steaming up the mirrors. When I slide inside the shower stall, which could easily fit five people, he's grinning, obviously pleased with his ploy.

"I'm just here to conserve water after all that," I say.

He nods thoughtfully at me and grabs my hip with one of his huge hands.

"Of course." The water sluices over his head onto me, and it's gloriously warm after the chilly feeling of taking off wet clothes. I step closer to him, and he presses me against the wall to envelop me in a scorching-hot kiss.

"Ralph deserves a prize," he says, sliding his hands down my wet body.

"He does, huh?"

"I get to make love to my wife. Of course he does," he says proudly.

"We should've taken pictures."

He stops nibbling my shoulder and looks at me. "Huh? You want a sex tape, babe?"

I laugh. "No, I mean Ralph, don't you think—"

"Though I adore the kids, I don't think this is the time to be speaking about him," he says, taking my mouth and thrusting his long, expert fingers inside me.

He kisses me deeply, savoring me, trying to figure out every dark secret I harbor. This man has a way of breaking me apart every time we make love, every single time. I come fast. My legs tremble, but I don't have time to think or react. He's lifting me, pushing me against the tile wall, and sinking his thickness inside my hot, wet channel.

We breathe desperately as he shatters me and puts me back together. I feel the sting behind my eyes when I realize this isn't just a fling. Not to me. I think I'm rapidly falling in love with my husband, and it's the one thing I wasn't supposed to do.

This was casual, temporary, only for one moment, and what am I going to do when it's time to leave him?

Chapter Thirty-Six

Caspian

DOGS—IN our case, puppies—as it turns out, are a great distraction to have in your back pocket. When you have regular posts about an incredibly cute dog and an adorable destructor—those would be Mia and Ralph—no one is really asking about how your marriage is going, which means a lot less scrutiny on Rys and me.

It also helps that the season is ramping up as we're gearing toward the playoffs, and we might end up fighting for a wild-card spot.

Rys seems to enjoy keeping up an Instagram just for the pups. She delights in the outfits and cute toys people send our way. The offices of the Orcas weren't too happy about receiving packages for us, now they're looking forward to them. Is Mia receiving a new dress, or will Ralph get a new toy?

Ralphie gets t-shirts, but they aren't as cute as the outfits the fans send to Mia.

Hadley had encouraged Rys to do the Instagram, and she had been reluctant since the pups are only temporary, but the chance to showcase the dogs on a larger scale and find them their forever home was a very good lure, it turns out.

Although… I'm starting to suspect she might be completely in love with them, and they might be a permanent fixture in our house. Heck, I'm a little bit in love with them too. When I'm on the road, I sometimes miss Mia and Ralph, wishing I had Mia in my arms and Ralph's warm fur as a comforting weight on my leg or lap after the game.

Instead, I have an empty, generic hotel room and room service food that tastes like cardboard.

Tonight's game was rough, physical, and grinding from the first puck drop. Even after an ice bath, my body is screaming at me. By this point in the season, we're all nursing a few injuries.

This year, I've actually gotten off pretty easy with just a lingering twinge in one of my shoulders most nights, but tonight I'd taken a bad angle into the boards and the twinge has evolved into a low, throbbing pain that even a massage couldn't dissipate.

There's not a lot I can do except settle in for the night in an uncomfortable sitting position, propped up by pillows.

Fern calls not long after I've settled on an ancient *Firefly* episode to lull me to sleep. It's strange enough that she's calling me after a game that I answer right away.

"Hey, Cas," I'm greeted not by Fern but by Elliot. My stomach drops unpleasantly.

"What happened?" I ask.

I jerk myself upward, which forces a hiss of pain out from between my clenched teeth. I force myself to settle back into position. I can't afford further straining the injury right now.

"Fern is fine," he says. "She just went into early labor this afternoon. She didn't want anyone to tell you until after the game ended."

I run a hand down my face.

Sometimes my family is too considerate of me and my games —they often put off telling me things until the season is over. You would think after so many years of playing, I would be used to it, but it still stings every time something is over, and I get a call like this.

It makes me feel superfluous to the family unit, although I would never tell them that. They think they're doing me a favor by not telling me, so I don't get distracted, and no amount of arguing with them will convince them otherwise.

"How is she now?" I ask.

"Resting," he assures me. "She did great."

"So, can we finally know if I have two nieces or two nephews?"

Fern didn't want to find out and Elliot, who's known for a while, refused to tell us.

"We have a beautiful girl and a precious boy. Elijah Joel McPhee was born ten minutes before his little sister, Alyth Ivy."

When I hear that my nephew is named after Dad, I can't help but smile. It fits that Fern uses his name.

"By the way, Fern had your game on the TV as soon as the nurses allowed it so I would know when it was okay to call you. She wanted to be awake for it, but the labor knocked her out, so she'll be out for a bit."

There's a warm curl of affection in my chest for my sister. She's going to be such a great mother. She's always looking out for everyone around her, already well-practiced in taking care of us.

"You want to see them?" he asks me. He's quiet on the other

end of the call. Everyone must be sleeping except for him. "I have them right here."

"Of course," I say immediately. I can feel my face stretching into a smile, the pain completely forgotten. "Show me."

He turns on his camera and waves to me before swinging it over to two small cribs with the tiniest babies I've ever seen. They're both swaddled tightly in striped blankets and look so delicate that I would be worried about holding them.

"That's Elijah on the left and Alyth on the right," he says. He reaches out the hand that's not holding on to the phone and gently rubs the side of Alyth's face with one finger. The baby, still asleep, grabs on to his finger and holds it tightly. He laughs, and I smile, relieved to see them so healthy and strong, even though a week before Fern planned to give birth.

"How long will you need to stay there?" I ask.

"Two or three days," he says, still quiet.

Elliot keeps the camera on the twins, and I watch them happily. I'd never really thought about kids of my own but seeing my sister's kids does stir something in me. For a brief second, I allow myself to wonder how Rys feels about kids before quashing the thought mercilessly.

"All things considered, everything seems good."

"That's great," I say. "Thanks for calling."

We stay on the call a little longer until one of the twins blinks awake and cries for—mom. Elliot hangs up with an apology, and I'm left alone in my hotel room again. I set the phone against my chest and sigh. I wish I could go straight home to see Fern and the twins in person.

I message Mills. He'll understand if I skip practice as long as I'm on time to play the next game. One of his mottos is family first.

Will Rys want to come and visit Fern? I know the last time she saw my family, they weren't very welcoming, but maybe this time it'll be different. This time I can say with a straight face that she's here to stay—if I can make her fall in love with me.

Chapter Thirty-Seven

Caspian

IN THE BEGINNING, Rys is reluctant about the idea of going to San Francisco to visit my sister and meet the twins. Though I can go alone, I want her to get to know my family better. They're different from the people she met when we first got married.

Do I understand why she's hesitant? One hundred percent. I don't blame her, and I don't want to force her either.

The last time we went to Santa Cruz, she felt as if my family almost ate her alive. It wasn't that bad, but they asked too many questions, and for an introvert like my girl, that's unacceptable. I tried my best to shield her, but I'm only one man.

Fortunately, she ends up agreeing to join me. This time, I'm sure they'll welcome her to the Spearman family.

And so I make the necessary arrangements so we can meet in San Francisco.

Lincoln drives her and the kids while I borrow my cousin's jet.

When I arrive at my apartment, Rys is lecturing Ralphie. "Shoes are not toys." She shows him a pair of blue suede Gucci loafers I hate. Well, one of them looks like a piece of blue corrugated cardboard. I want to say, "good boy," but since she's educating him, I stay quiet.

Rys shows him his turtle. "You can chew on this. Do we understand each other?"

Before Ralph can agree, Mia notices me and prances to where I stand. I bend to pick her up, but of course, her brother has to be the first one to slobber all over my face. He loves to get attention. I pet them both and snuggle them close to me.

"He has FOMO," Rys protests. "And by the way, I hope you weren't in love with these shoes because…well, they're gone."

"You're in trouble, big boy." I ruffle the top of Ralph's head and do the same with Mia. Laughing, I walk to Rys, closing the space between us. "Mom gave them to me for Christmas. I think I only wore them for New Year's?"

"Hi," she greets me.

"I missed you, beautiful," I murmur just as I take her into my arms and kiss her. "Did you have a good flight?"

"It was interesting," she says. "The kids didn't love the fact that they had to be in their kennels. Next time I might get them a couple of sedatives to make the trip less stressful for them."

"Thank you for coming with me." I press her close against me. I had no idea I missed her this much until I have her in my arms.

"It's important to you."

"We should go to the hospital and then maybe take the kids to Uncle Aslan's place. He has a big backyard."

"That mischievous grin doesn't give me any reassurances. We're not taking them to a place where they might cause trouble just so you can irritate your brother. He already hates me."

"First of all, he doesn't hate you. No one in my family does."

Well, that's not exactly true. No one, except maybe my mother, but that's just because she thinks my wife is a gold digger, and she's upset because I refuse to introduce them. After Heath spoke to Lysander, Aslan, and Gatz, they all said it'd be best to keep Rys away from her.

When I asked Elliot to let me know when Mom was visiting the babies, he told me she wasn't invited to see them. Fern warned her that until she went back to therapy, she won't be allowed to meet her grandchildren.

I haven't asked Gatz if Mom has met Soleil, I assume she has, but then again, I didn't know there was an issue between Fern and our mother.

"You went silent. They hate me, don't they?"

I shake my head. "No. It's Mom. We have to make sure we keep you away from her."

"Why?"

"She's intense."

Rys stares at me for several seconds before saying, "I get it."

The tone is unsettling, but I don't read much into it. I have enough things to worry about. I clap. "Well, let's get ready so we can head to Santa Cruz to meet the babies."

When I call Elliot to confirm Fern's room, he tells me the babies are doing great, and the family was sent home a day earlier. Aslan and Keaton let us leave the kids with them before driving to Santa Cruz to meet Alyth and Elijah.

"Rys, it's so nice to see you again. I hope my brother is treating you right. If not, call me, and I'll remind him how to behave," Fern says, walking toward her and giving her a big hug. "I didn't know you'd be here today, but I'm glad. The last time you were here I was too exhausted to contain the savages. My brothers can be quite irritating. I apologize."

"How are you feeling?" Rys asks, ignoring what my sister just said.

"Tired. No one warned me these two would ignore the schedule I set up for them. They hate sleeping at night or when I'm trying to rest. Luckily, I have an army staying around to help us."

I arch an eyebrow. "An army?"

She gives me a smile as if saying, right, I forgot to tell you about our current plans. Fern is the one who keeps me updated about everything that's happening with the family, except the pregnancy has taken a lot of her energy, and I've been too busy with Rys to reach out to her. We probably need to correct that. I'd hate to grow apart not only from her but the entire family.

"Well, Cory, who I think is sleeping, took time off from the company and the bar to help us. Benedict, Atzi, Heath, and Teagan, Elliot's niece, are here too. They've been a godsend. I don't know what we'd do without them."

Rys is the one who stares at Fern and asks, "Benedict is here?"

I'm not surprised that Benedict Farrow is here. He's not only one of Heath's closest friends, but he's also part of the family. In a way, we adopted him when he moved from New York to Stanford to study medicine.

"Is there a problem with that, Rys?" Ben steps into the living room.

She takes a step back. "You're here?"

"Of course, I'm here. They're my family." He looks at me. "Really, I told you to stay away, and you married her?"

I shrug. "What can I say? She's pretty irresistible."

Ben shakes his head. "No, just no." He looks at Rys. "Have you talked to Avery?"

"Yeah. Have you?"

"No, she's mad at me because I didn't tell her about your relationship." He huffs. "There wasn't a relationship to begin with, but even if I was allowed to talk, she wouldn't believe me."

I'm glad I contacted him and warned him about the wedding, the media hounding us, and the narrative we're using. He wasn't happy, but as he told me, he has my back.

"So, when can we meet the babies?" I ask because the last thing I need is to discuss Rys with the family.

Fern checks her watch. "Probably an hour. They should be waking up in thirty minutes. Hopefully, Elliot will be back by then. He went to check on a construction site which isn't too far from here."

Fern looks at Rys. "Why don't we get you something to drink and you can tell me all about the puppies? I'm dying to meet them."

As they head to the kitchen, I sigh with relief. Fern has welcomed her, which means Rys is officially a Spearman. I just need to convince her we're meant to be together.

Chapter Thirty-Eight

Rys

Yesterday was unexpected.

All of it.

I think that's what I get when I'm around Caspian. There's never a dull moment, and thankfully, all of them were good moments, not like the last time I met his family. The twins are adorable. Watching Caspian with them made my ovaries explode, and my biological clock demanded I have a few Spearman babies.

Of course, I won't.

Am I falling in love with him?

I can't deny it, but the season is coming to an end, and as much as I'd love for this fairy tale to continue, I was reminded by Benedict that I don't belong. It's not like he implied it, but I watch him and Heath's friend, Atzi, be part of the Spearmans. They fit so perfectly with the rest of the brothers and sisters.

Well, except Ben isn't trying to be a friend to Cory. As I said, yesterday was pretty eye opening. Avery is right, Benedict is just friends with her. I've never seen him look at her the way he looks at Cory. He treats her as if she's a goddess. And maybe the last time we were in Paradise Bay he came along to see her, and not to spend time with Avery.

Sadly, I also learned that I could never become one of the Spearmans. I'm barely a Holland.

Dad keeps to himself. His family never includes us. Mom… well, my mother is another story. She's always keeping herself away from everyone, including her family. Milly and I are close, but now that she has Ernie and the kids, she only needs me to babysit them or to keep our mother away from her.

Still, everyone was welcoming and warm toward me. Keaton and Aslan asked me about adopting Mia. I told them she's not ready yet, but as soon as she is, they'd be the first ones to learn about it. Though, I warned them that we're going to try to find a house that'll receive Ralph and Mia.

I hate to admit Leyla was right, it's going to be hard to find them a home. However, Aslan and Keat didn't say never mind, but will they be open to adopting my big boy too?

This morning, Cas suggests we head to Jane's for breakfast. It's a small restaurant in Pacific Heights. I accept immediately. Since I'm in town, I plan to take the kids with me to check on the animal hospital.

"Shouldn't you be training instead of having breakfast?" I joke.

He shakes his head. "Not yet. I have a couple more hours before I have to be in Portland. Are you sure you don't want to come with me? We can have fun in the airplane—become part of the mile-high club."

I wouldn't mind saying yes. My entire being aches for Cas when he's not around and needs him when he's close. I'm going to miss him.

He caresses the base of my neck with his knuckles. There's something about him that makes my insides quiver with just a slight touch. I want him to take me to his apartment and make love to me before he leaves. It's not like we didn't spend all night naked, making up for all the time we've been away from each other. Yet, my body is still needy for him.

"This is how you think you're going to beat my team, *Captain*?" I move my gaze to find Thad Roderick standing right next to our table. He nods once. "Polaris, it's nice to see you with your husband. How's the marriage?"

I glare at him. It's on the tip of my tongue to remind him I go by Rys, but I don't waste energy on him.

"Go away, Roderick," Cas orders, waving his hand toward the exit.

"Why? I'm here to see my good friend Caspian Spearman and his lovely wife. Isn't that what your people claim?" He leans closer. "Except, we're not friends, and you fucking stole *my* girlfriend. That's the truth. Since you couldn't get a spot on the Sharks, you decided to take my girl? How are my sloppy seconds?"

"Shut the fuck up!" Cas stands up.

"Do you have any idea what your publicity stunt created?" Thad turns to look at me. "Was it worth it to drag Cameron through the mud? She's innocent. Now her life is upside down because of you."

"Me? You were sleeping with your best friend."

"It's what I need when I'm between games. You never put out. What was I supposed to do? I wanted things to work out for us. I tried, but you only wanted your five minutes of fame."

"This isn't about fame. And I recall you begging her never to leave you again—but she will. You're not who she loves."

Okay, I'm still being petty but he's ruining our breakfast.

"Maybe it's not fame but a way to get to me because I chose her and not you." Thad points at Caspian. "He's only using you to get to me. Has he told you why he hates me?"

I turn to look at Cas, who glares at Thad.

"We used to be friends. Best friends. It was back when we were both in college." Thad grins. "We shared girls back then, and it seems like we still share them. But that's not why he loathes who I am. He wanted to be on the Sharks, but I got the spot. Not him."

"You bought the spot," Cas clarifies.

"If that's what helps you sleep at night, let's go with your version. See, that's the thing, you can't accept I'm better than you. Did you think stealing *my girlfriend* was going to hurt?"

Cas smirks with satisfaction. "I hope it does. You're missing one hell of a woman."

That air of victory in his face feels like a punch, I'm having trouble gasping for air. Is he using me?

"It doesn't hurt at all. She's replaceable, but I have a proposition for you. I'll give you my spot on the Sharks in exchange for her."

Cas looks at him as if he's considering it.

I freeze, my fingers clutching the paper napkin in front of me. My eyes stare at the man who just a few minutes ago was making me feel like the luckiest woman in the world. I can barely breathe as I wait for him to say something, anything.

Thad laughs and looks at me. "That tells you how much you mean to him—nothing. He's just playing with you. Hockey and his family are his life—you are just like every other woman in his life, temporary. Why do you think he never shares his private life? I've seen the way he treats them. You're like a princess today, tomorrow you'll be picking up your shattered heart."

"Shut up!" Caspian growls.

"Oh please, at least be honest with her. Rys here is just a scapegoat. Does she know about Frankie and *your* son? How are they, by the way?"

Cas's eyes glimmer with frustration. I, on the other hand, am having trouble keeping up with this conversation while trying to keep my heart safe.

He has a son?

That's something he should've disclosed during at least one of our conversations. I haven't seen any pictures of the boy around the house.

Is he hiding him? Was he just another PR issue his family erased?

I wouldn't be surprised; wealthy people usually lose touch with reality and think people are just disposable. Children, wives…anyone.

Thad gives me a thorough glance. "You'll never measure up to her, sweetheart. If I were you, I'd walk away before he breaks your heart, the same way he's done to others."

Then, the asshole pouts. "Aw, you thought you were his special snowflake. Sorry, but as Cam said, you're not that great."

His words don't affect me, it's Caspian's silence that's slowly destroying me. I can hear it; my heart is breaking. It's shattering the same as a piece of fine crystal carelessly tossed from the tallest building.

But I don't show any emotion. I'm good at pretending too, and so I plaster a smile on my face. "Oh, Thad, this is too petty, even for you. It's time for you to grow up and learn how to lose. You wanted to have us both, Cameron and me, but as I told you, that's not for me. Now, I hope you're done with your tantrum because it's time for us to go."

I take my purse and walk toward the exit. My legs are shaking, but I don't let that stop me.

"Rys." The agony in Cas's voice makes me come to a complete stop as soon as I'm out of the restaurant.

I turn around and smile. "Is everything okay?"

"Are we okay, babe?"

Babe? He dares call me babe after what happened inside? He's usually pretty good at putting me first but obviously he has his priorities, like hockey and…is his son even important to him?

It doesn't matter, I need to keep my cool. "Sure. We knew this was bound to happen. He likes to draw attention to himself and play the victim. You should've accepted the position in the Sharks. I had no idea you guys were that close."

"We—"

Since I don't plan on speaking to him again, I ask, "Was it Frankie or the Sharks that broke your relationship with him?"

He stares at the floor. "It's complicated."

"I'm sure it's not. The answer is hockey, isn't it? You wanted that position in the Sharks."

"I did. Dad loved the Sharks. We spent a lot of our time together watching games, even going to other states to cheer them on. At twenty-one, it destroyed me that I couldn't reach that dream."

"Who was Frankie?"

"A friend with benefits." He sighs, avoiding my gaze "It was ugly between the three of us—"

"Stop," I order, because I don't want to know more.

I'm done. He's everything I hate. I thought he was open and loving and…he's nothing like the guy I was falling in love with. A part of me still wants to believe what transpired in Vegas between Cas and me isn't related to Thad, but after hearing everything that happened between them… I just can't keep up this farce.

"Rys?"

I look at my watch. "I have to go to the clinic. They're expecting me."

"Can we talk?"

"Later," I say, already pulling out my phone and calling an Uber.

"Let me drive you there."

I finally look into his eyes and say, "Sorry, but I need some space. That display was too much for me."

He nods as if understanding. "Rys, I—"

"We'll talk later, okay?"

Thankfully, the car arrives. I climb in without looking at him. If I do, I might not be strong enough to say goodbye.

Chapter Thirty-Nine

Caspian

SHE LEFT ME.

Rys dropped my sorry ass without even saying goodbye. Not only had she upped and left, she disappeared from the face of the earth.

It's been almost a month since the last time I saw her, and what am I supposed to do?

I feel like my life is over.

And yet, I have to continue pretending that I have energy to play hockey and lead my team to the Stanley Cup finals. By some miracle, we're in the playoffs. The past few weeks without Rys have been a blur, and yet, there's still some hope for the Orcas.

It's to no one's surprise that the fight with Thad and what everyone thinks was my breakup with Rys is still trending on the internet.

Let it go, people.

It's old news!

So what if I wanted to beat the shit out of Thad Roderick when he interrupted breakfast with the wife? I didn't do shit, and maybe that's why I lost her.

My PR is thankful that no one caught the audio, but everyone can see on those viral videos that the three of us were fighting.

I know that people are starting to talk about my lackluster performance. Of course, they're blaming it on Rys. When questions about my personal life come up, as they inevitably do when reporters are probing me for reasons I've yet to score in this series, I keep my mouth shut just like Lang told me to.

Nothing I say about the situation will make it better or bring her back. Besides, it's still so raw that I'm not ready for anyone else to know. Pathetically, I keep hoping I'll come home after a game and Rys will be there waiting for me like nothing ever happened.

But that's the thing, isn't it? Nothing did happen. I've gone over and over it in my mind, and I can't find anything that would have triggered such an extreme flight response from Rys. We always talk about everything, she listens. She believes me.

Roderick said a lot of shit from our past, but we could've discussed it. I can open up about Frankie and the kid.

Why just leave?

Okay, maybe I should've been more assertive during that conversation. I stayed in the back and let him insult my wife. It's probably all the PR training.

Did I want to move to the Sharks when he offered?

Fuck.

No.

I'm not a twenty-one-year-old boy trying to reach for some dream his father had. I'm not only loyal to my team, but I would never trade Rys for anything. I should've said something, but again, I was trying to prevent a PR nightmare.

Do I regret my behavior?

So fucking much. It's been too hard to breathe without her.

Yet, the playoffs are in full swing and there's nothing I can do but be the captain of this team. I'm sitting in the locker room after a brutal game 5 when I get tapped for press. I make my way out to the table set up with microphones and a room full of reporters.

"Spearman, tell us what went wrong tonight," is the first question lobbed at me. I give the reporter a blank look. I know they're all just looking for soundbites, but how annoying can you get, seriously?

I shrug at him and say, "We just didn't have our heads in the game tonight and got outplayed."

"What will you say in the locker room after a night like tonight?" another guy asks.

It's hard not to roll my eyes. These reporters are always looking to write the next *The Mighty Ducks or Miracle* movie or something—they act like we're all one inspirational speech away from glory.

Tonight, I don't even have the patience to pretend it's not a dumb question. I just want to get home to Ralph and Mia and crash into bed.

"Not much to say." I smile sarcastically at the reporter when he clearly expects me to continue.

He gives me an unimpressed look back but cedes the ground to the next man up. It goes on like this for another five or six minutes before they give up on me and I'm released.

I towel off my sweaty head and go back to the locker room. It's grim inside. Everyone is pissed about tonight. It was a total blowout, and we needed the win. We're not out yet, but we'll be playing for our lives in two days' time.

I'm throwing the last of my things into my gear bag when Spacey slides up next to me and pats me on the shoulder.

"Everything all right, man?" he asks.

I shrug at him and shoulder my bag.

"You headed out?" I ask, instead of answering.

He purses his lips but nods and follows me down the tunnel toward the basement-level parking garage.

He walks beside me all the way to my car even though I can see his obnoxious orange Camaro in the next row over. He leans against the driver's door, so I'm blocked from getting in. I pop the trunk from my keys and stow my gear bag away while he watches me.

"You know you can talk to me about your fight with Roderick and the…are you two getting a divorce?"

I face him with raised eyebrows. Which fight? The one at Jane's in San Francisco, or the one we had an hour ago on the ice? The Pacific division comes down to Sharks vs. Orcas, and so far, we're both losing. Mills, the owner, called me last night to remind me that this isn't a personal vendetta.

Why can't I beat the shit out of Roderick while on the ice? Okay, I know the answer, and I have to do better for my team, but it's too fucking hard.

I might've lost the love of my life because of Thad Roderick.

Did I lose Rys?

Are we getting a divorce? I want to fix things between us, there's still hope. I sigh and cross my arms. He holds his hands up as a sign of peacemaking.

"I'm here for you, Cas. Just putting it out there. I care about you, and not just because you're playing like shit right now," he says.

"Thanks," I say dryly.

"If you need someone good at emotions, I'm sure Shelly would be glad to help too," he continues. "She likes Rys."

"It's not about Rys," I practically growl at him, but he barely blinks. He's seen a lot worse from me.

"No?" he asks, a shit-eating smile sneaking onto his face. He's really asking to get punched, isn't he? Guess he didn't get enough from the Sharks tonight. "Must be your family, then? The cute puppies that you definitely aren't adopting and keeping forever?"

"Spacey," I say, at the end of my patience. "Get off. I'm going home."

He sighs and knocks his knuckles against the shiny black door of my car.

"Alright, fine," he says. "But get your shit together before game six, okay? We need you out there, bud."

I grunt at him and swing myself down into the car. I'm peeling out of the parking spot almost as soon as the engine revs up. I can't get away from all these questions fast enough.

During the drive I came to the realization that it's over and I need to move on.

Even though I'm dead tired and need as much rest as possible, I take a trash bag and put all of Rys's clothes and other things she brought over in it. Mia and Ralph follow me around the house as I do it, whining.

"I know, but she's not coming back," I tell them and then immediately feel stupid for trying to reason with them.

I head to the kitchen, give them dental chewies, hoping that will distract them, and put the bag by the front door. Maybe I can get someone to send it to her, wherever she is, because clearly, she doesn't want anything to do with me.

She quit her job, cleaned out her apartment, and...she disappeared. Not even Lang, who can find anyone in the world, has been able to track her. I don't understand.

I collapse into bed and, after staring at the ceiling wondering if she ever felt anything for me, I fall asleep.

I'm awake with the sun since I didn't bother to close my curtains, and when I stumble out into the living room, the first thing I see is that stupid garbage bag. I sigh and walk over to it before picking it up. I take it over to the couch and carefully extract everything. A lot of clothes, an empty laptop bag, and some other things like a curling iron and a magnet she'd brought home once. One by one, I put everything back where I'd found it the night before.

I'm not giving up. I made that mistake once; I won't do it again. I'll find her, I just need to get my guys to the Stanley Cup. It's not that I don't care about her, but I need to finish one thing before I put all my energy on the most important person in my life.

I don't want to half-ass it and lose her forever.

Chapter Forty

Caspian

I SKATE HARD from the first puck drop in game 6, determined to make this one count. I finally break my scoring drought with an assist from Jonesy at the end of the second, and it feels like pure adrenaline when my linemates crash into me on the ice.

The game stays tied at two apiece for the rest of regulation, and we face down our first overtime with a stupid penalty kill that wouldn't have happened if we weren't all so tired.

As soon as our man is released from the box, I take a shift change and collapse onto the bench in exhaustion, trying to catch my breath. Coach is double-shifting the top two lines, trying to scare up a goal, and it's taking its toll.

I take in big gulps of air, and someone pats me on the back before throwing me a fresh water bottle. I pour half of it over my head and the other half in the general direction of my mouth.

Then, it's my shift again. It goes on like that for what feels like an eternity until the buzzer goes off, indicating the end of the overtime period. In a regular-season game, this would mean the relief of a shoot-out, but in playoff series, we keep playing until someone scores, which means another grueling overtime period is coming our way.

I skate off the ice to take our short break and scarf down as many calories as I can to replenish some of the energy in my body.

We're back on the bench before any of us are ready, and the offensive coach tries to talk through a few plays with the top line again. I clap my right-winger on the back and nod at Jonesy, who is always on my left. We know more than any fan that what happens in overtime is more often luck than skill because we're all so exhausted, especially this late into a physical series, but that doesn't mean we can't be dialed in.

"Let's do this, boys," I tell them before skating to the face-off dot.

To my displeasure, it's Roderick across from me. He sneers at me, obviously just as displeased.

"Pretty pathetic this series, Spearman," he says, just out of earshot of the ref. "Barely potted one goal, and now you're about to lose. I heard you lost the girl too."

I bare my teeth at him, but otherwise, don't take the bait. It pays off, and I win the face-off, knocking the puck over to Spacey, who takes off with it toward our end of the ice. I race to catch up with him and cycle the puck for as long as we can until Jonesy finally takes a shot. It clangs off the bar and bounces back into play. I drive forward and just barely get my stick on it to toss it back toward the goal when I see Roderick coming up quick on my right.

The puck goes in, but before we can celebrate, the wind is knocked out of me and I'm on my back on the ice. The world spins for a moment, and I realize someone must have barreled into me well after the whistle. I grunt and try to take inventory of all my limbs. My shoulder is on fire, but that's nothing new. I wince when Spacey pulls me up and then hugs me.

We've won the game on the Sharks' barn, so the crowd is booing us as we leave the ice, but the victory is still pretty sweet. I wait until I'm well into the tunnel before sidestepping out of the line and flagging one of the trainers, Abrams. He runs to me with a towel thrown over his shoulder and frowns.

"You went down pretty hard on that last play, Spearman," he says.

"Yeah, no shit," I say. I clench my teeth and count backward in my head. No sense in being a dick to our people. I open my eyes and he's completely unaffected, giving a rapid-fire order to one of his staff. "I think it tweaked my shoulder."

Abrams's mouth presses into a grim line, and he nods.

"Alright, first of all, let's get it iced," he says. He snaps at one of his other staff and points him toward the media availability area. "Hey, kid, tell Hadley that Spearman won't be available tonight."

"Yes, sir," the younger trainer says and scampers off immediately.

I exhale in relief.

"Thanks for that," I say. "Might be better than the pain meds you're gonna give me."

Abrams clucks at me and uses his towel to wave me in the direction of one of the tiny rooms set aside for our staff. I start stripping off my sweater and pads, but pretty quickly, it becomes obvious that my shoulder isn't going to allow me to actually maneuver them off and over my head.

"I'll cut it if I need to," Abrams says behind me, but before he takes scissors to the sweater, he gives it a quick jerk and it comes free of my head. I hiss in pain through my teeth, but I've felt way worse. Nothing's broken. I can tell that much. Probably just a tendon or muscle that needs to be reworked and soothed with an ice bath or two.

Abrams hands me a tablet with some clips already on it from our tape guys.

"You see the hit yet?" he asks. "That motherfucker, Roderick, took his time getting to you, didn't he?"

I watch a clip of the hit on the small screen and curl my lip at it before putting it aside. It had been a late hit—a very late hit. That's how he'd gotten me so thoroughly disoriented.

"Wouldn't be surprised if he gets himself a nice suspension for that one," Abrams mutters. "We can only hope."

"Anything that takes him out of game seven would be good news for us," I agree, although I suspect he'll probably just get a wrist slap and a hefty fine. He's a league darling, motherfucker or not, and the Player Safety guys seem to love him because they're always letting his bullshit slide.

Abrams checks me out, and I pass his immediate mobility checks well enough to get some ice strapped to my shoulder and pushed off toward the locker room.

"We'll take care of the rest once we're home," he says, sounding almost as exhausted as I am. The adrenaline is starting to fade, and I'm sluggish as I go through the motions of a quick shower and pulling on some clean clothes, even as my shoulder screams at me. As soon as I'm dressed, I down the pain pills that Abrams gave me. They kick in fast, and by the time the team bus is ready for us, I'm almost asleep on my feet.

Someone helps me on the team plane and then I sleep until we're back in Portland a couple hours later. I'm still hazy when we get to the airport parking garage, but there are multiple hired cars waiting for us. It's so late it's actually early, and there's no way I could drive, so I gratefully sink into the back seat of one of the cars after giving my keys to a valet who will drive it to my house for me.

Chapter Forty-One

Rys

THINGS HAVE BEEN PRETTY bad since I left Caspian Spearman.

Bad as in I live wrapped in a blanket, eating ice cream on the couch, and watching every game Cas plays just to see his face. I'm pretty sure I've eaten more ice cream in the past month than I have in the past two years combined.

Dad's the only person who knows where I am—his house. The only time I'm out of my room is when there's a game. The

Orcas are playing the Sharks, which has a twisted kind of symmetry to it.

Thad seems to be out for Cas's blood on the ice, and Cas... Cas doesn't seem to even really be on the ice. He looks miserable and is playing even worse. I'm trying not to think about my role in all of this. It's not like I can magically make it all better now either.

I miss Mia and Ralph a lot, and my job. I applied to several positions, but all the clinics—two—in this small town have said the same. We don't have any openings. If I could only see my furry kids, things wouldn't feel so crappy.

Their social media account is still getting updated regularly with pictures I don't recognize, so Cas still has them, which is a relief. I hope Mia and Ralph stay with him forever.

"Rys, I love you, but you can't live with me for the rest of my life," Dad says as he enters the kitchen.

"I know."

"What are your plans?"

"I'm waiting for the playoffs to be over."

"Why?"

"Everyone who loves hockey is trying to figure out where I am, because apparently, I broke *Cassie*."

He arches an eyebrow. "Your husband?"

I groan because I have to start the divorce proceedings. Leyla offered Pierce's services when I quit. She even told me to go to Luna Harbor to open the new branch. It's so remote no one will ever know I'm there. I quit, but she swears I'm just on vacation until I'm over my broken heart.

"Listen, I love having you here, but you can't hide forever."

"Why didn't you and Mom work on your marriage? I mean, you're a great father, but apparently you were a shitty husband."

He chuckles. "I didn't meet her expectations."

I stare at him dumbfounded. All this time I expected one of them to confess that Dad had a mistress, or some fetish Mom couldn't live with but... "What does that mean?"

He shrugs. "I never understood either. Nothing I did was

right, I guess she wanted a Ken doll to do what she said or... I don't know. No matter what I did, I couldn't be the husband she wanted me to be, and one day I just left."

You don't just leave a marriage, you fight, you compromise, you remind yourself why you agreed to spend the rest of your life with that person. And I swallow hard, because isn't that what I did, run away when I saw that something might hurt me?

Actually, learning more about Cas shattered my heart. I fell in love with my husband and he...

I look at my father. "Did you love her?"

"With all my heart, but I couldn't keep up with her toxicity. I chose to be a good father to my children and hoped she wouldn't make you believe marriages are like fairy tales. There's a lot more after that happily ever after. You have to work at it, and sometimes one or both partners will make mistakes. It's up to them to fix them—together."

I nod as if understanding.

"Do you love this Spearman guy?"

"Yes, but I didn't fit in his world. He seemed so perfect, loving, but then he'd choose everyone else before me. It was a matter of when he'd push me away, so I chose to—"

"Run before you got hurt?"

"Something like that."

He gives me a sad smile. "That's always been you. You'd rather not deal with the real world, feelings, or rejection. I blame your mother."

"Why?"

"It's like when moms warn you about the dangers in the ocean. Sharks, jellyfish, waves...they build so much fear in your mind that you choose not to ever go into the ocean. She's been feeding you some sort of hate-fear for men and love for years."

I frown. Is that what happened?

Ever since she divorced Dad, she keeps telling me how bad men are, and how I'll get hurt if I open my heart or my legs. I think about all the calls and texts she's sent me since I left for college. I remember the panic I felt when I was finally comfortable with Cas.

Was that it?

I was just waiting for him to fail so I could leave?

I left when my heart felt danger?

"Love is worth fighting for," Dad says, glancing at the television. "It's like a hockey game. You didn't score this game, but the players don't give up. They work harder and make sure during the next one they beat their opponent. It's about improving, learning, and being there because you love it."

It seems like my father knows more about love than I thought. "Why are you single?"

He gives me a sad smile. "It's not for the lack of trying, but I guess a lot of people live in fear just like you. I've dated plenty, but no one special enough to keep forever."

"Are you lonely?"

"No. I have my two beautiful daughters, my grandchildren… maybe one day I'll get to meet the furry grandchildren."

"Cas and I…"

"Try talking to him before losing him for what could be the rest of your life, Rys."

I stare at him, unsure of what to say.

Is it worth it?

Is Caspian Spearman worth it?

Chapter Forty-Two

Rys

DAD not only agrees to come with me to game seven. He pays for the tickets—ice-level tickets—the plane tickets to Portland and the hotel rooms. I get to pay for the beer and hot dogs.

The plan...okay, there's no such thing as a real plan. I'm hoping by the end of the game I'll text Hadley and ask if she can let me into the locker room to talk to Cas. It's a long shot, but it seems like something he might like.

He always asked me to go to his games, I didn't do it often because of fear. This is me putting myself out there, trying something new, for love.

Of course, when I set up this plan, I wasn't counting on the fact I'd be sitting almost next to his brothers and sisters. Even Fern is here with her husband. Thankfully, the couple with the little kid who sits next to me doesn't know who I am. At least that's what I think. The friendly woman next to me keeps wanting to start a conversation.

So far I've learned her name is Hannah. She has two children with a third one on the way. Her son might be six or seven? His name is Lucas and her husband's name is Alex. Though Alex and Lucas are so into the game they didn't even wave when she introduced them.

She has a daughter, Jyn, who stayed in Seattle with her parents.

Don't get me wrong, she's very nice, but keeps asking me questions. I do my best to avoid answering them. Who goes to a hockey game to make friends?

All I try to do is keep up with the puck for most of the first period. Mostly I go by the grunts and hisses beside me to gauge how things are going, and I obediently stand when the goal horn goes off and the fans all yell, "LET'S GO, ORCS." I do the accompanying fist pump even when it feels slightly ridiculous.

By the end of the first period, the Orcas are winning two–nothing. Cas scored the first goal and assisted on the second. During the first intermission, a waking nightmare happens when the cute little promotional video with Cas and me playing around plays.

I freeze in my seat and crouch into as small a ball as I can. I claw at Dad's arm, and he laughs, watching the video.

"Uncle Cas," the little boy next to me yells, pointing at the video. "Can I see him now, Mom?"

"Not yet, Lucas. We need to wait until the game is over."

My eyes open wide. Great, this is Hannah, Cas's cousin. No

wonder she was trying to be friendly. At least one of the Spearmans doesn't hate me.

But why am I so close to them?

"What the hell?" I whisper, even though there's no way anyone can hear me. Not even Dad.

This is just perfect. And then, I just have to watch a much happier version of me make a fool of herself on the ice...

I stare at it longingly. God, Cas can really give good hugs, can't he? I finish off the last of my beer and stand up. Self-conscious or not, I'm going to need something stronger than a light beer to get through this.

While I'm out of my seat, I also buy a baseball cap to go along with a very strong gin and tonic from the concession stand. I chew on the tiny straw that came with it as I gauge whether it's safe to return to my seat. The hat gives me some sense of security, although it might just be in my head. It at least feels like my face is a little more hidden.

I wait until almost the last second before scrambling back to my seat. No one stops me or even looks too closely as I slide in because they're all too focused on the impending puck drop. Well, no one but Heath, who's now sitting next to me. He smiles at me, and Atzi, his best friend, waves.

Our gazes are back on the ice. It's Cas and Thad at center ice again at first, but the referee forces Thad to trade places with one of his teammates.

I hold my breath. It had been Thad who knocked Cas down late in the last game, and I had to wonder if it was on purpose.

It certainly looked like it was on purpose in the dozens of replays the broadcast had played of the whole sequence, but the league had only fined Thad instead of a suspension, so apparently, it wasn't as serious as it could be.

The game is back. This time it's Cas who scores a goal. The commotion in the arena is contagious. He's playing like he hasn't done it in the past few weeks. The game resumes and my eyes track Cas on the ice for a while.

"I wish you had showed up a few games ago," Heath

mumbles, and I take my eyes away from the ice for a second but go back when he flinches.

That's when I spot Thad knocking through other players like a bowling ball and he seems to be spoiling for a fight.

It's while I'm tracking Thad that there's a commotion in another corner of the ice, and I turn my head just in time to see blood smeared on the ice before realizing it's Cas at the bottom of a pile of men who must have collided with the boards. I'm standing before I even think about it.

The other two men, both Sharks, stand up and skate off, but Cas isn't getting up.

The guy next to me stands up, touching the glass, anxious to get to Cas, and I realize it's Heath. The couple that was near me is now on the other side, hanging with the rest of the Spearmans. A trainer runs out onto the ice in a low crouch to check on Cas.

"He's going to be okay," Heath assures me, squeezing my shoulder.

"I…"

Heath smiles. "We're just glad you're here—"

The silence in the arena interrupts him. My heart beats fast with anxiety.

It looks like Cas isn't responding to the trainer, and the Orcas form a wall around him, blocking the view entirely. It's a couple of minutes before they part, and my knees go weak to see that Cas is up with an assist from one of his teammates and skating by himself off the ice, albeit very slowly. The arena claps for him as he leaves the ice.

It's only because Dad gently pries the cracked plastic cup from my hand that I realize I've clutched my drink so hard that I cracked the plastic in two, and my hand is covered in sticky gin alcohol.

I barely blink at it as I look back to where Cas is now hobbling through the boards. Although he'd been skating on his own, as soon as he's off the ice, his shoulders slump a little and one of the men standing by slips an arm underneath his and props him up.

Cas goes down the tunnel.

"I'm going to check on him," Heath says to everyone around.

"Can I come with you?" I almost grab on to him.

He shakes his head. "I'll text you once I know what's happening, okay?"

Heath never texts, and Cas doesn't return for the rest of the period.

Chapter Forty-Three

Caspian

"Rys," her name slips out of my lips like a plea. "What you...here?"

She recoils from where her hand had clutched the thin paper bedding underneath me. She crosses her arms instead, and I want to reach out for her, but none of my limbs will cooperate. They all feel full of lead, which must be the painkiller they gave me. I frown and shake my head, trying to clear it, but it remains stubbornly foggy.

"I should… I can go," Rys says, but she isn't talking to me, or at least I don't think she is.

"You should," the familiar voice of one of my brothers says. "He's got enough to deal with right now."

I want to argue—I can't think of anything I want more than for Rys to be here—but my mouth doesn't cooperate with my brain's commands either. Instead, I blink a few more times before everything fades out to a static.

When I next wake up, I'm in a hospital bed in an empty room. There's a huge cast on my leg which answers at least one question. It doesn't look like I'll be getting out of bed without assistance anytime soon, which is unfortunate because I really need to pee.

I look around for my phone and am grateful to see it lying on the plain aluminum bedside table. It's awkward to reach it. I have to shuffle over and stretch my arm, but I knock it a little closer so I can grab it. I'm just debating who to call when Heath bustles into my room.

He yelps when he sees me awake and then sets down the coffee cup he had in his hand.

"Cas," he sighs, and he sounds relieved. "They said you probably wouldn't be awake for another hour or two. Let me call the nurse."

I groan, but I know better than to argue with him. Instead, after he presses the call button, I gesture at my cast.

"What's the verdict, doc?" I ask.

"Compound fracture in your femur and some tearing of your meniscus," he reports. "Hayes Aldridge operated on you. He said it could have been a lot worse. He'll be back tomorrow to check on you. We decided to take you back to San Francisco so we can keep an eye on you. We're setting up everything in the penthouse so you can recover."

I want to stay in Portland, with Rys, but will she want me back?

Today we were supposed to talk about us. When Lang got me what could be my last hope—her father's number—he said she wanted to go to game seven, and so I got them tickets and made it happen.

Of course, Thad had to go and fuck this up for me—again.

"And the game?" I stick to safer subjects.

He makes a "pfft" sound. "Obviously, you guys won. You'll be up against the Wild. Well, not you. You're out of commission for months, probably."

I scowl at that, but the huge immobile cast on my leg makes it hard to argue. He pats me on the arm in sympathy.

"Aslan, Gatz, and Lysander will be by soon," Heath says, glancing at his phone. "Fern is at your place with Elliot and the kids."

I make a face. "You guys don't have to take rotations. I'll be fine. I have people I can call."

He punches me on the arm this time. "We're the people you can call, asshole," he says. Then, sobering, he adds. "By the way…"

"Yeah?" I ask when he hesitates.

"Rys was at the arena when you got hurt, and she was sent away," he says.

I frown at that. "So it wasn't a dream?"

"Nope."

"Who sent her away?"

He stares at my cast.

"Heath?"

"Aslan. He said he talked to her."

"Why did he send her away?"

"I think, and this is just a theory because I didn't ask, but there's a rumor spreading that Thad was out to get you because of her. They want her away from you."

"That's not… I fucked up. She left because I didn't defend her while the asshole was insulting her. I haven't told her about Frankie either."

He rubs the back of his neck. "I know, you've told me that a million times, but you haven't told them what happened with her. Sorry I wasn't there to stop them."

"This was… I was supposed to win the fucking game and ask her to forgive me for fucking up, not—" I groan.

"You need more meds?"

"No. I need her. Can you…" I swallow and look away. "Would you mind calling Rys?"

"Okay, but I'd keep her away from the triplets. If you're planning on some grand gesture to get her back, be prepared to fight them."

"They can go fuck themselves," I say, and confess, "I love her, you know. It hurts so much to be apart. A lot more than having your leg broken."

He smiles at me. "Finally, you're admitting to being in love with your wife. I mean, we knew it, but you seemed like you were trying to keep it a secret from everyone—even her. Maybe she can play nurse while you recover."

I just hope she forgives me.

Chapter Forty-Four

Rys

"IT LOOKS like Caspian Spearman will be out with a lower-body injury for the duration of the playoffs, leaving the Portland Orcas without their captain. Now, he's usually one of their top scorers, but he was actually pretty quiet in this series against the Sharks, only netting four goals and three assists for the entire seven-game series. Kyle, how do you think this will impact the Orcas as they take on the Minnesota Wild?"

The TV drones on, but I turn off the sound after the scant update on Cas. After his brother made it clear I wasn't welcome at the arena, I'd left as quickly as I could, catching a rideshare out of there and texting Dad that I would meet him at the hotel.

We'll fly back tomorrow evening to Vermont. Since then, I've been waiting by my phone, hoping that Cas might call with an update, but it's been frustrating radio silence, which I suppose is fair play in return for what I've done.

At some point at night, I fall asleep. When I check my voicemail, I'm legitimately floored to hear Heath's voice. "Hi, Rys, it's Heath. Cas asked me to call you—I think he would have himself, but he's still pretty loopy on painkillers."

I clutch my phone to my ear when his voice drops a little. "Listen, I don't know exactly what Aslan said at the arena, and Cas doesn't remember it at all, but I hope you know our older brothers are pretty protective. All that to say…whatever Aslan said to keep you away when you were obviously concerned, don't take it too much to heart.

"Oh! Cas is out of surgery—obviously—and they were able to correct the break. He's going to be in a cast for a few months, but he'll be okay. Um, yeah, that's all. Hope we can talk soon. I think Cas would really like to hear from you, for what it's worth."

I can't stop myself from replaying the message just to make sure I didn't hallucinate it.

"Cas would really like to hear from you," haunts me as I pace along the hotel room. I'm glad Dad isn't here to watch me lose my shit.

When my phone rings again. I dive for it, but it's not Heath or Cas. It's my mother. I groan but pick up the call.

"Well, thanks so much for deigning to talk to your mother," she says when I answer.

I roll my eyes and flop onto the bed.

"What's up?" I ask, trying to keep the annoyance out of my voice. She rarely calls if she doesn't have something specific she wants to say—we're not really a chatty family.

"The internet thinks you've separated from your husband," she says. "Did he do something? Cheat on you?"

My jaw twitches in annoyance.

"Mom, I don't really have time for this right now," I say. "But no, he didn't cheat on me."

"But you are separated?" My mother can sniff out a lie by omission like a bloodhound can find bodies in the woods.

"Physically? Yeah, because I'm at home, and he's in the hospital," I snap at her. "I'm actually on my way there right now to see him, if that's all right with you."

She sniffs as though she's really injured by my tone, and my hand grips the phone a little tighter. I realize with a jolt that there's nothing I want more than to actually be on my way to the hospital to see Cas right now. I sit up, feeling a little disoriented, and look for my purse. It's been kicked under the couch, but I fish it out, still holding my phone to my ear.

"Why is he in the hospital?" she asks, finally sounding just a tiny bit sincerely worried.

"He got injured in a game," I say. "Last night."

"Oh, that's right, he does play hockey, doesn't he?" She laughs as though talking about some beer league he plays in. I grind my teeth together and rub my nose as I throw on some shoes and check my appearance in the small hallway mirror.

"Yes, Mom, he plays hockey," I say, suddenly too tired to argue with her. "And I'm going to see him. Because we're married, and I love him."

My mom will have no idea how much I actually mean that last sentence and the way it stabs me right in the chest to say it and wish with all my heart that it can still be a reality for us. I hear Heath saying, "Cas would really like to hear from you," in my head again, and nod to my reflection in the mirror, determined.

"I have to go," I say to my mom and hang up on her before she can drag me into any other conversations about the gossip on the internet. I text Heath's number and ask him where the hospital Cas is staying at is.

Heath: *He was discharged earlier today—Ben and I will be taking care of him in San Francisco, but we won't move him until next week. In the meantime, we're at your house.*

I exhale as I read the message, and then with shaking fingers, I open the app to request a car. I just hope that when I get there, I'll be allowed inside.

Chapter Forty-Five

Caspian

"Hm, hope you're up for company because someone just pulled into the driveway," Aslan says, craning his neck from where he's sprawled in the armchair. I'm just about to turn and look, expecting to see a teammate or someone else from the Orcas, when Aslan whistles. "Oh, and she dared to show up."

My neck snaps in that direction so quickly I hiss in pain at the way it pulls my torso. I keep forgetting I need to consider my leg and battered body before moving in any direction.

"Let her in," I tell my brother when he doesn't immediately get up.

He's grinning at me as he very slowly gets up and saunters to the door. He opens it several long moments later and I hear him say, "I might not, and there's nothing you can do to stop me."

"Hi." Rys sounds hesitant, and I hate that.

My throat seizes with all the things I want to say, but Mia and Ralph have realized who is at the door and start barking loudly.

Rys corrals the puppies. She picks up Mia but has trouble catching Ralph, who is almost bigger than her at this point, and she laughs when he jumps on her, scolding him gently as she puts his paws back on the floor.

I drink her in the whole time. She hasn't seen me around the corner yet, and I want to treasure these last few moments where I get to see her unguarded.

My brother says something in a low rumble, and Rys suddenly turns her head in my direction, locking eyes with me. She's still bent over Ralph, but she gives him one last pat and straightens up. She's flushed and fidgeting and looks prettier than I've ever seen her before. I wish I could stand up from the couch and sweep her into my arms.

"I'll, uh, leave you guys to it," Aslan says, his eyes mischievous as they dart between Rys and me. He clicks his tongue at Ralph who is still splayed belly-up on the floor. Ralph throws himself to the side and rolls over to standing before shaking himself and trotting happily after my brother, who has grabbed his leash. He gives me an exaggerated wink as he clips the lead on Ralph's collar. "I'll take the big loop."

"Go," I tell him, my eyes still on Rys. I'm concerned she'll disappear or run the moment we're alone, but she's smiling gently at Aslan and waving goodbye. The door shuts behind him, and she looks back at me with slightly panicked eyes. She puts her hands in her jeans pockets and walks slowly toward where I'm marooned on the couch.

"Hi," she says again, but this time just for me.

I swallow, suddenly overwhelmed.

"Rys," I say, my throat scratchy with emotion. "You're here."

"Yeah…um, I wanted to be there during surgery, but…" She sits in the armchair Aslan just abandoned. I wish she was so much closer. "I hope it's okay that I came."

"I've missed you," I say, getting the words out there before I bite them down again.

Some of her nervousness melts, and she smiles at me.

"Yeah?" she sighs, her shoulders dropping. "I've missed you too, Cas. I… I came to your game to talk to you actually. I don't know if you know, but I was there—"

I grin. "I might've talked to your dad a couple of times, and he let me know he was looking for some tickets."

"You knew?"

"I've been looking for you. Lang gave me your dad's number, and thankfully he was willing to give me a chance—your mom not so much."

"She's…" Rys sighs. "You talked to Dad?"

I nod. "Yeah, you were pretty hard to find. I wanted to apologize for what happened—"

"I shouldn't have run." She nods, then shakes her head like she can't decide what to do.

"It wasn't your fault. The moment was too overwhelming. Instead of being your husband, I slid into player mode and became polite… Listen, everything he said is true." I exhale.

"Why do you hide your son?"

I chuckle. "Well, everything except that. Thad and I were best friends in college. His parents have money—not as much as my family, but they like to spend it on whatever their only son wants. Their daughters don't matter as much to them, it's pretty pathetic. The point is, we were competitive, I thought it was in good spirit, until it wasn't.

"I'm ashamed to admit we shared women. Back then, I was a stupid kid who didn't think about anyone's feelings, not even mine. Frankie…she was a friend. We had fun and were close. Thad thought I was in love with her."

I pause, staring at the window, then back at her. "As I said, she was a good friend. However, he decided to take her away from me. I had no idea that's what he did, grabbed what he thought was precious to me.

"Frankie was collateral damage. She got pregnant—with his child—and his parents tried to make her lose the kid. She asked me for help, so I helped her. Roderick took it to heart and told everyone I knocked up *his* girl.

"My family hid the mess, for her, not for me. We helped Frankie, and since then, Roderick likes to pin him on me. It was ugly, and when I went to Vancouver, to the farm team of the Orcas, they kept me there until the fucking rumors died down and I was clean."

"You could've told me about…" She presses her lips together. "Is Frankie still a part of your life?"

"She's not important. I didn't see the point of mentioning her, and yes, I get Christmas cards from her. She has a beautiful family, but that's all. When I saw you in Vegas, I was upset Roderick had been an asshole to you—but not surprised. I wanted you to forget what happened, in case you were heartbroken."

"I wasn't," she mumbles. "Not then, but when you two were fighting, I felt like you were using me just to—" She stares at her hands. "It scared me to be in love with you because you're so out of my league."

I clear my throat, looking for words to express what I feel, but the emotions are too big to fully hang on to. I look at her instead. Her usually shiny hair is limp around her face, and the circles under her eyes are almost as dark as my own.

"Babe, you're the one who is out of my league. You're a smart, strong, independent woman who heals animals. I'm just a fucking hockey player whose career might be over."

"You'll be fine. Everyone loves you, and your bones will heal. How are you?"

"Better now that you're here," I say, meaning it sincerely even if it's a cheesy line.

She meets my eyes, and I can't help but reach an arm toward her, wanting her to come closer. She looks at it hesitantly but then slides off the armchair and onto the carpet until she's sitting cross-legged on the floor beside me. She takes my hand into her lap and twines our fingers together.

"Cas," she says seriously. "I hated to be apart from you, but I hate it more that I feel as if we don't fit. When it's just the two of us, everything is incredible, but then we're outside in the real world and you change so much."

I squeeze her hand. I can't help holding my breath until she finishes. I have a horrible spark of hope in my chest now, and her closeness only stokes the flame.

"I want real or nothing at all. I can't be married to a man who can't be himself once he's out the door," she says finally. She bites her lip, looking down at her own hands. "I hope that's something you want too."

"Rys," I say her name when she doesn't look up at me for a long time. I smile at her. "The truth is, I'm an introvert that's good at pretending I can be social. I'm not a jock. I'm a chemist, just like Lysander. I pretend to just like to be in the tasting room, when in truth, sometimes I mix grapes with him, and we try to come up with a new kind of wine.

"More importantly, I love you, and I want us to have a real marriage with our messy dogs, our crazy families, and maybe along the way a few children."

"Cas," she whispers my name.

"You're gonna have to come up here so I can kiss you."

She huffs a laugh, and a few tears escape the corners of her eyes. I wipe at them with my thumb as soon as her face is within reaching distance. Her lips are soft and dry when they press against mine, and it's perfect.

We're perfect for each other, and even after so many mistakes, I know we're going to be okay. This is it, the beginning of us.

Epilogue

Rys

THE ORCAS WIN the Stanley Cup.

Cas isn't there to play, but he doesn't miss any of the games. We watched them from the team's suite. By the last game, I know all the plays and every move the guys make and even yell along with Cas, who keeps back-seat driving the team. During the parade, his teammates carry him around as if he's the MVP.

Thad Roderick only gets a slap on the wrist for what he did

to Caspian. A five-thousand-dollar fine and a four-game suspension that will carry to the next season isn't enough, but there's nothing I can do. I just hope karma fucks him where it hurts.

After ten weeks with the cast, Hayes Aldridge removes it and sends him to a physical therapist in San Francisco. We pack our things and move to San Francisco for the off-season. Of course, Lysander complains that he broke his leg on purpose, so he doesn't have to help around the vineyard.

Cas believes it's Lysander's way to hint that he should retire and come work with him. However, Caspian isn't ready to change careers. He believes he has at least a few more years as a captain if the Orcas extend his contract next year.

As for me, Leyla gave me my job back under the condition I'll never leave her again. Unless I decide to start my own practice. So now, I'm back working in San Francisco during the summer. I'll be traveling to Portland once a month. Our relationship keeps growing. I've yet to introduce Cas to Mom though. And I haven't met his mother either.

He doesn't know what's happening with her, but Lysander told him to keep me away, and he plans on listening to him—it might be the first and only time though.

This weekend, we traveled to Baker's Creek to visit his orthopedic surgeon and the most important thing, to sign the paperwork.

"So it's official?" he asks Leyla as he holds Mia close to his chest. "They're ours."

Leyla extends her hand. "It'll be fifty."

"Oh, I didn't know we had to pay. Do you accept credit cards?"

"No, I mean Rys owes me fifty dollars. I told her she was going to keep them. We even bet on it, and here we are signing the documents of Mia and Ralph."

Cas laughs. "Pfft, you really took advantage of her. I knew the moment I saw them, she wouldn't give them away."

"Right, but she swore they were just temporary."

Cas looks down at me and kisses me. "I think we have to go

over the word temporary. It doesn't mean forever. I mean, we're yours forever, but you shouldn't tell people the wrong word."

I stick my tongue out. "Come on, babe, it's time to go home. If we're lucky, we'll be able to drive to Santa Cruz today. I promised we'd babysit the twins tomorrow."

"You're a sucker for babies and puppies."

He wiggles his eyebrows. "We should practice making some babies. Maybe by the time I retire, we can have a few. I'll be the stay-at-home dad."

And he'd be the best at it. "I guess we're leaving. Thank you for everything."

Leyla hugs me. "I'm glad everything worked out for you and that you're finally happy."

I smile at her, realizing that she's right. I'm elated because I'm next to the man I love. No matter where we land or what we're doing, we're together. Since we reconciled, he's been more himself and less the guy he likes to personify for the fans.

Maybe we made a few mistakes along the way, but my favorite one was marrying him.

A year later…

Cas

"So let me get this straight. You want us to marry again?"

The arena is full. Everyone is celebrating our second win. Not many teams win the Stanley Cup two years in a row, but we did it, and I'm hoping we do it again next year. However, as promised by Mills Aldridge, the owner, if we won, he'd let me propose marriage to my wife.

I know it's a year and some months late, but it's never too late to tell the woman I love that I want to spend the rest of my life with her.

"Babe, no pressure, but you have two teams and an entire arena waiting for an answer."

She is doing that cute thing she does, sucking on her bottom lip and looking at me with those crinkled brown eyes that make me fall in love with her again and again.

"Tonight is supposed to be about you, not me."

"This is about me. I want us to renew our vows. This time I won't make the mistake of livestreaming the wedding or hiring Elvis to sing while I tell you how much I love you. We'll even invite the fam."

She laughs and leans closer, whispering in my ear. "Well, the thing is that I have a surprise for you—at home. This feels like a good moment to tell you though, that we're expecting a baby."

I stand up and lift her from the floor, pressing her against me. "Are you serious?"

"Yes. As I said, this was your day. You're going to be a dad."

"I fucking love you so much, Rys. I do, so, so fucking much."

"Well, ladies and gentlemen, you heard it from the source. Our favorite couple is having a baby. I guess our captain really knows how to score."

If I wasn't too happy, I would flip off the announcer, but I put all my energy into kissing my wife. The love of my life and the mother of my child.

Excerpt

I hope you enjoyed Along Came You.

Keep reading for an excerpt of Faking the Game, a snippet into Aslan's story. A look at Can't Help Love, Gatsby's and also My Favorite Mistake—Caspian's story, releasing on October 4th.

Faking the Game

Aslan

It's past three o'clock in the morning, and I'm standing at my living room window.

Some would say I have insomnia. That's not the case. I operate on very little sleep, just like my father did.

Nights like this, I enjoy staring at the city lights, the Golden Gate Bridge, and the dark sky. If I were in my childhood home, I'd be gazing at the blanket of diamonds illuminating the blackness above us. That's the beauty of Paradise Bay. The sky is always clear. There's no light pollution dimming the stars.

If it wasn't so late, I'd drive forty-five minutes to my old house and see if that would bring me some answers to all the problems I'm dealing with lately—including my mother.

While growing up, I watched my father doing the same thing almost every night. He'd be staring at the big picture window that looked toward the vineyard. I guess I got my restlessness from him. Some nights, he'd wiggle his fingers, calling me to approach him. We would both stare at the still sky for a long time.

I was an active kid, but those nights when he invited me to be next to him, I didn't fidget or say a word.

"I'll let you in on a secret," he said one time, whispering. "When in doubt, always ask the stars. They'll listen to your problems and will guide you until you find the right way to solve them."

And here I am, as I do almost every night for the past fourteen years since he left us. I stand in front of the window, hoping to find a star that can guide me. Joel Spearman was an extraordinary father, a wise man, and a kind soul. I can't understand why he left us so soon.

It's been too many years without him. Anyone would think that I would be over his death, but I'm not.

He was too young, too full of life and plans.

I rub my chest as if trying to calm the ache of my soul—it's impossible.

The searing pain of losing my father will never disappear, and on days like today, it becomes unbearable. I needed him then and I need him now.

We barely survived his loss and everything that happened during those dark days.

It all started with the vineyard. One night, my family was woken up by the angry flames burning the vines and the guesthouse. According to the fire marshal, it was arson.

Two days later, Dad died of a heart attack. He was found in the field. According to Mom, he had gone out to assess the damage. It wasn't until supper time that she sent my brother, Heathcliff, to look for him. Heath is the one who found him lying lifeless next to the burnt vines.

If that wasn't enough, I found Margie, my fiancée, fucking my cousin Troy during Dad's funeral.

She taught me a valuable lesson. Women only want me for my money—that's exactly what she told Troy as he fucked her. Since then, I haven't dated or taken anyone seriously. My sister Fern says it's just an excuse to be an asshole like the rest of the men in her family.

Is she right?

That's debatable.

It shouldn't matter if I'm dating or not.

But it matters to my mother.

That's why a year ago, I lied and told her that I had a girlfriend. It's the best way to keep her happy. Mom lives in this enchanting world where true love exists, and soulmates are paired before they're even born. According to her, it happened to all the Spearmans and it's bound to happen to her children too.

Someone should remind her that her soulmate died fourteen years ago. I can't understand how she still believes in that nonsense. She hopes my current girlfriend is *the one.*

My brothers and sisters hate that I've been lying to her for the past year, but it's worked like a charm. Unless I count those days when she wants me to bring my mysterious girlfriend to our family dinners—or for family celebrations. Like the Spearman family reunion happening in less than two weeks.

Yep, I'm fucked.

Hey, I never said the plan was bulletproof.

Should I have had a contingency plan when I learned about this event?

Nine months ago, when we learned about the possibility of a Spearman reunion in Hawaii, I laughed with my brothers, Gatsby and Lysander, my triplets. They've been my partners in crime since the day we were conceived. Our logic laid on the fact that the Spearman family is huge. Dad was one of seven children. Each one of them had five to eight children. Some of them are parents too. It's impossible to get that many people into one place.

We were wrong.

Three months later, I received an invitation to the first annual reunion. They had invitations and we had to RSVP.

The event is well organized. I found out that my cousin June, who used to own a PR company, is one of the master-minds behind the entire operation. Her twin Jeannette and her sister-in-law, Emmeline, are helping her. Those women could take over the world on a weekend and fix it if they had more time.

Since then, Mom has been reminding us that we need to RSVP and our presence at the event is *mandatory*.

With less than two weeks to go, I have to figure out a way to skip this trip. Am I afraid that my mother will drag me against my will? Yes. I think she's capable of that and much more.

Do I want to go?

Maybe.

It's Hawaii. My cousin Jackson and his wife Emmeline will be renewing their vows. Jack is the oldest of our generation. His brothers and sisters are my favorite cousins from the Spearman side, but Mom wants me to bring my girlfriend—after all, we've been together for more than a year. Plus, I'm in the middle of an acquisition, a merger, and…there's a lot of work to do. I can't just pack up and take a vacation.

There's also the fact that a week after this trip is over, we'll be celebrating the fifteen-year anniversary of Dad's departure.

I should borrow a page from Gatsby's life and disappear for a few weeks. Good luck finding me while you're celebrating nonsense or remembering that we lost the most important man in our lives.

"Fuck, I need drink."

As I'm about to head to the kitchen for a glass of scotch, my phone rings. I groan as I realize it's Lysander's tone. So much for having a peaceful night without dealing with family. I take one last look at the Golden Gate Bridge and turn toward the kitchen. If I'm going to deal with him, at least I'll do it with a finger of scotch on the rocks.

I pull out a tumbler, the bottle of alcohol, and answer the phone, setting it up on speaker. "What's up, asshole?"

"Some of us would like to get some sleep," he growls.

If I wasn't pouring my drink, I'd be staring at the phone. Why the fuck is he calling me then? "Good night? Go to sleep? Do you need a nighttime story? Did you try closing your eyes?"

"I can't sleep because you're thinking too fucking loud."

I burst into laughter, almost dropping the glass. "Really? You're complaining about my loud thoughts?"

"Yep, plus, you make too much fucking noise. I heard you when you left the bed and went to the kitchen. Why are you back there? Do you need another drink? We should soundproof your apartment so I can sleep."

I look down and give him the finger. Letting him and Gatsby live in my building was one of the worst decisions I've made in the past couple of years. They don't pay rent, they come to my apartment at all hours of the day to take my food, and I don't have any privacy. "Or, hear me out...you can move out of my building. It'd make more sense to live close to the vineyard."

He laughs but doesn't confirm what we know. Lysander doesn't want to live near Mom. He doesn't need to live in the guesthouse. Why can't he just buy a property or rent a place in Paradise Bay?

I guess because he'd be so close to our mother, she'd be barging into his place every five fucking minutes. *Mom needs a hobby* I think as the amber liquid goes down my throat.

"What's upsetting you?" he asks.

People think he's the most relaxed of the triplets, but that's Gatsby. Though, in all honesty, none of us are chill or calm. The moment Dad died, the burden of the family fell onto us. Suddenly, we became parents to our younger siblings. Life came to be complicated as we tried to parent five teenagers and our mother, who had situational depression—losing Dad hit her pretty hard.

That's the part of her situation I don't understand. She suffered so much when she lost Dad. Why would she want that for her children? I wouldn't want anyone to go through what she went through just because they thought they were in love with me.

"Listen, if you're just calling to harass me—"

"It's a courtesy call to check up on you," he interrupts me.

"I'm fine."

"I call bullshit. Something is either frustrating you or causing you major anxiety. I just want to help you chill the fuck out. Have you tried hooking up? Releasing endorphins is a healthy way to relax."

"So now you want to dictate how I feel?"

"No, I want you out of my head and heart. It's so fucking hard to deal with your feelings, Gatsby's feelings, and my life."

I snort. "Because you don't have feelings."

"Ha, don't start playing 'let's annoy the fuck out of Lysander because'…I hate being a triplet."

Is it wrong to enjoy his frustration? Probably, but I swear it's so fucking funny when he's annoyed.

"Can you just tell me what's wrong with you?" he growls.

I know when to push, but I also know when I have to back off. Since the game is over, I confess what's fucking with my head. "Hawaii, our mother, the merger…why can't things be simple?"

"Tell Mom, 'Fuck off. I don't need a wife. The only girlfriend I have is the inflatable doll Caspian gave me for Christmas.' See, it's pretty easy."

Fucking Caspian and his gag gifts. He's such an idiot.

"I don't understand why she's always on my case and not yours. She has seven children *other* than me to nag, and I only hear her say, 'Aslan, dear, when are you going to get married?' Why?"

"Margie," he answers.

I close my eyes, exhaling harshly. "It's been over for fourteen years. Again, she has seven other children to harass."

"None of us have ever been close to having a family. You were engaged."

"You—"

"I don't count," he interrupts before I say something else. "Listen, your only options are to confront her or keep going with your fabricated girlfriend."

He doesn't understand that I'm at a crossroads. This is it. The fable has to come to an end. Unless he has a solution. "How can I continue with the lie?"

"Take *that* girlfriend to Hawaii, you can break up with her during or after the trip."

"She's not real," I reminded him, annoyed.

"It's not a matter of having her but finding someone to play the part. Hire someone for the week."

"Sure, let's bring a whore to the family event. Classy."

"I meant—"

"You're an idiot," I interrupt him before he says something more stupid.

"Hire an actress."

I'm about to pull out my hair. Is he serious? I snap my fingers. "Why didn't I think of that? I could just post it on Craigslist. Actress needed to play the part of my girlfriend. Must be available to travel. No passport needed. Non-smoker, not clingy, nothing serious. I'll have my assistant run it before noon."

"The hot VP of Operations could do it."

"Keep Keaton out of this conversation," I growl.

"Aww, you don't want us to mention your favorite, shiny, unwrapped toy?"

I've no idea what he means by that, but I'm about to go downstairs and rearrange his face.

"You've always had a soft spot for her. On the plus side, she knows how to deal with your...lovely personality."

He's not wrong. I consider his idea for one hot second. Can I fake being with Keaton? She's smart, fun, and beautiful. Not that I'm gawking at her every time we're in the same room. Okay, I might glance at her from time to time because, well, she's gorgeous.

"Do you think that's going to keep Mom away?"

"At least for a few months. It's perfect." He snaps his fingers, almost as if he just had a brilliant idea. "She's leaving San Francisco in a couple of months, isn't she? You can claim that *she* didn't want to have a long-distance relationship."

The thought of her leaving makes my stomach drop. Soon, she'll move to Arizona—*if* the merger with Monti Media goes as planned. Another good reason why I have to skip the reunion. This is her dream, I have to make it happen—for her. I can't go on vacation.

But what if I bring her along? We could work in the hotel room, pretend we're together, and enjoy a week in Hawaii. She needs a vacation. I hate to admit that this plan might work, but am I that desperate?

No. I don't mix business with pleasure or family.

Including Keaton in this insane plan isn't the solution. "There has to be another way?"

"Yes, but you don't like to confront Mom. Hence the big lie, Pinocchio."

"I'll tell her I'm too busy to go to Hawaii."

He chuckles. "The last time you tried to wiggle your way out of a family event using work as an excuse, she threatened to fire you. She might not hold any shares for the company, but she's my mother, and if she asks, I'll vote in her favor. Everyone would agree with me."

The board is a joke. My brothers and sisters only make decisions that are convenient for Mom, and I have to deal with the rest. "I love our mother, but she makes our life too fucking complicated."

"I couldn't agree more. Now can you settle down? I have to be at the vineyard in less than two hours."

"You need to move back to Paradise Bay."

"I will, as soon as you tell Mom to fuck off."

That's probably going to be never.

>>>> Continue Reading Faking the Game

Can't Help Love

Maia

Fourteen years ago...

"Your plane ticket for May is ready," Dad says.

I stare at the screen, trying to concentrate on the conversation. It's impossible.

I've always been a rational person.

At least I think I am. My parents raised me to keep my feet firmly planted on the ground. I follow all their social rules. *All* of them.

Well, at least I did up until I started my junior year of college and finally moved out of the house—and the state.

Dad is a very conservative man who believes women shouldn't leave home until they get married. According to him, I'm not allowed to have a boyfriend before the age of twenty-five.

Ha, good luck with that, *Papi*.

"Maia, are you listening?" Dad growls.

Oh, I'm listening. I just can't build a coherent sentence.

My secret boyfriend is hiding under the table—as I requested. However, he's doing very naughty things while waiting for this call to end.

I swallow a whimper as Gatsby licks my left thigh as he skates his hands down the center of my body. He's so close to my core I can't breathe. I'm desperate and needy for him.

My story is simple. I'm a naïve good girl who went off to college and discovered she liked sex—a lot. It doesn't help that my boyfriend can't keep his hands to himself. He's always touching me, and I'm always wanting it.

I blame him.

Damn it, Gatsby Spearman and his delicious mouth and wicked fingers.

I told him to hide and stay quiet while I'm speaking to my parents. What is he doing?

He's quiet, but also being his usual wicked-horny self.

"You said your last test is May fifteenth, the ticket is for the twentieth. You're staying in San Diego for the summer, right?"

I bite my lip and nod a couple of times as Gatsby slides his finger between the elastic of my panties and touches my already soaking slit. I jolt but contain my expression. Every evening, this man does something forbidden while I have my daily video call with my parents. By now, I can keep my face stoic and my voice almost steady.

If computer science doesn't work, I might have a career as an actress.

I try to kick Gatz, but he holds my legs in place while pushing two fingers inside me.

Deep.

So, so deep, I can't help but open my legs for him and hold on to the table so I don't fall.

My breath becomes shallow, and then, I sober up when my father speaks. "Maia, are you paying attention to us?"

"Of course, I'm paying attention, *Papi*. You have my ticket for M-May."

"Are you okay, *mija?*" Mom asks.

I nod. It's almost impossible to talk when my boyfriend's thumb circles my clit in a torturously slow motion while two of his fingers thrust in and out—fucking me.

"Of course, I'm okay." I swallow hard.

Mom nods, satisfied. "How are your midterms coming along?"

I hold the table tighter, gulping down a breath as Gatsby keeps tormenting me with his fingers, his mouth. He's about to send me to the edge, make me come so hard that my screams will be heard all the way to Europe. I'm trying to hold still, but it's almost impossible.

My traditionalist parents would be very disappointed in me if they realize what's happening under the table. They'll be dragging me back home if they learn that I lost my virginity last September—it was my boyfriend's twentieth birthday. We spent a romantic weekend on Tybee Island.

They'll hate knowing that we have sex several times a day. We sleep in the same bed almost every night. They wouldn't approve of our relationship at all.

Dad will buy a chastity belt, throw me in my room, and ground me until I'm thirty. Since I'm not planning on dealing with the consequences of Gatsby's actions, I look under the table and mouth, *Stop it.*

Gatsby gives me a wicked smile. Not only that, he dares to pull down my panties while giving me a challenging glare.

"Stop," I whisper.

"End that call." The commanding low voice sends a wave of heat through my entire body.

I'm getting close.

So close.

"Are you okay?" Mom's voice makes me hit my head on the table.

"I hate you," I whisper.

Gatsby winks at me. "It's okay. I have enough love for both of us."

And I melt.

Getting under the table and riding him would be ideal, but I restrain myself and go back to my conversation. The one I plan to end soon so I can go back to my boyfriend.

"Are you okay?" Dad asks, giving me a suspicious glare.

"I thought I saw a cockroach under the table, but it was a wrapper," I lie.

Mom touches the bridge of her nose. "Where are your glasses?"

"In the nightstand."

"You should wear them all the time. That's why you think that your trash is an animal. Clean the studio."

My studio is clean, Mom. My boyfriend is a neat freak.

I almost roll my eyes, but I don't. "*Si, Mami*. I'll do that this weekend."

"If you have a pest problem, call the management company. They'll take care of it," Dad reminds me.

"I can squash bugs, *Papi*, but I'll keep that in mind."

And just because he can, Gatsby pushes my legs wide, dipping down. I feel his breath against my wet center. When he swipes his tongue against my clit, I shiver. Pleasure rising like a tide of euphoria. His mouth is so good, my breathing is becoming ragged. If I don't end this video call now, they're going to hear me come.

"I don't want to cut this short, but it's time for me to go back to studying. Say hi to Tiggy and Cee-Cee for me."

Dad glares at me. "We barely spoke. Your sisters plan on saying hello after they finish their homework."

"Maybe you should give me one of those things called…cellphones. I could text even if I'm in class." My parents are thrifty. They don't like to spend on superfluous items. Someone should tell them that landlines are becoming obsolete. It's been almost a decade since the last century ended.

"We'll see," Dad answers. That's his polite way to say, *no*.

"I'm sending you a care package tomorrow. We made *polvorones*."

"Thank you, Mami." I wave, ending the call and closing my laptop.

Pushing my chair away from the table, I spring out of the chair. "What is wrong with you, Spearman?"

He's still on the floor, grinning. "Have I ever told you that you taste delicious?" The dirty boy licks his lips and sucks on the fingers he had inside me a couple of seconds ago.

"You're a wicked man. If my father knew about this"—I point from me to him a couple of times—"he'd kill you and ground me forever."

"Your parents love me."

"No. They liked you when we met you because you helped us carry the boxes and furniture while moving. You were also charming."

"I'm still charming."

"They'd stop liking you the moment they learn we're dating, and once they learn we're…doing it, well, they'll hate you."

He gets out from under the table, and I notice the silhouette of his hard length pushing against his shorts. "I hope you know we're not having sex tonight."

"But I just got started, and you're so wet… I think you're ready to ride me." He gives me a sweet, pleading look. "It's our lucky charm. We have sex, and we pass tests with flying colors."

I can't remember when he decided that he'd fail if we didn't have sex the night before an exam.

Like he needs an excuse. We're humping each other every chance we get. I'm not complaining, but he should at least own that.

Crossing my arms, I give him an unamused look. "We have a

presentation tomorrow, not a test."

"It's sixty percent of our grade," he reminds me, and suddenly his smirk appears. "You know what we should do? Move this party to my apartment. Your studio is cute but small."

I give him a defeated glance. I'd agree if my parents were different, but they're overbearing, and I can't disobey them. This might be the day they call me or... I don't want to tempt my luck.

Gatz automatically takes me into his arms. I rest my head on his chest, listening to the beat of his heart. It's soothing. Though I want him to finish what he started during our call, I can just stay here, in his protective embrace.

"Can we go to my place?" he insists.

"Nope. If they call and I don't answer, I'm doomed. If they catch me out of my studio after eight, my parents will drag me back to San Diego—immediately."

"I think you're exaggerating."

"You don't know Mom and Dad."

"I've met them. They're lovely. They'd know me better if you didn't hide me every single evening. It's a pain to keep quiet when this place is so small."

"Sorry? There's not much I can do to fix it. You knew what you were getting into from the beginning."

He sets his chin on top of my head and sways me as if we're dancing. "Let me get you a cellphone so they can reach you at any time—in my big-ass, comfortable apartment."

"No, thank you."

"Every time I offer to buy you something, you decline it."

"Why would you buy me stuff? You're lucky I let you pay for my meals. May I remind you I'm an independent woman?"

"I don't know. Margie never says no to Aslan. Actually, she's always demanding something new."

Every time he talks about his brother's girlfriend, I get the feeling that she's a gold digger. Maybe I'm wrong. After all, I don't know her. Aslan, Gatsby, and Lysander might be triplets, but they sound like totally different people. I wish I could meet them. Maybe one of these days I'll accept his invitation to visit his family.

"Well, I'm not Margie, and you're not Aslan. I'll get a job over the summer and buy myself a phone."

He releases me and puts his hands on my shoulders, staring at me with worry. "Hey, don't stress out. We'll keep sleeping here and I'll hide. All I want is for you to be happy. I love you, Little Blue."

Every time he calls me that, my heart flails wildly in my chest.

Is it normal to feel this way about a man?

I don't know. I was homeschooled all my life. I took several classes at the community college, and it wasn't until I turned eighteen that my parents agreed to let me leave the house. I moved to Atlanta, where I now study at Georgia Tech.

If my parents had a choice, I would've gone to Stanford or Caltech. Unfortunately for them, they didn't offer me any scholarships. I look at Gatsby and smile because he is one of the best things about my college experience—if not *the* best.

He's not only the best boyfriend in the world. He's my rock. From the moment I arrived on campus, he held on to my hand and helped me adjust.

And best of all, he loves me as much as I love him.

He kisses my nose, brushes my lips with his. "What are you thinking?"

"That I'm lucky to have you, and maybe we should practice tomorrow's presentation."

"We already did that thrice. It's time to take a break."

"I just want it to be perfect. As you mentioned, the majority of our grade is riding on it. What if we fail?"

"Last semester you said the same about the app we created, *Rencontrer*, and we aced it."

I smile. "You know we could start our own matching company. I mean, not right now, but if we set up the website, tighten the algorithm, and come up with a good marketing campaign... My graphics for the branding are pretty awesome."

"You're brilliant and a kick-ass artist, but there are more colors than purple, pink, and blue..." He pauses, kissing my nose again. "We'll talk about that when we're ready to set up our company. I'm sure Dad will back us up, and if not, I'll use my trust."

"First of all, we're not taking money from anyone, I want it to succeed on its own merit. Also, we need romantic colors for the application." We might be years from starting it, but I want to get things started.

"That's because you're a romantic and believe in all that stuff."

"You don't?"

"I believe in you and that I'll never stop loving you."

The insecure girl inside me asks, "Is that a bad thing?"

He hugs me again, tightening his grip. Then, he pulls us forward. We fall on the fluffy queen-size bed.

The one he bought—against my wishes—last September, after the first night he stayed with me. He claimed the single bed my parents got me was too small. Okay, he was right about that. The guy is six-three and has the body of a swimmer. He's a combination between Johnathan Rhys Meyers's face and Michael Phelps's body—including the washboard abs.

"No, loving you is never a bad thing. I'm hoping that after we graduate, we'll set up *Rencontrer* and everything else we come up with together. They'll be the best applications in the world."

"Sounds like you plan on keeping me around a long time."

He brushes some strands of hair away from my face. "Forever if you allow it, but let's not get sidetracked. I think you owe me something."

He lowers his head and kisses me. As always, his mouth burns my lips, and the heat combusts my entire body. I sway on the edge between fantasy and love.

>>>> Continue Reading Can't Help Love, Gatsby's Story
https://claudiayburgoa.com/wp/cant-help-love/

Along Came You

Elliot

We all think there's a defining moment that shapes a person's future.

There's not *one moment.*

It's a series of events that occur throughout our lives.

The person I was yesterday isn't the same as I will be twenty years from now.

Not many guys think about the happily ever after when they're young, but I'm pretty sure that I happened to meet the love of my life at the tender age of two. I don't think I can say that I fell madly in love with her. We just loved each other. I believed she was my future and my everything until not one, but several events changed our lives.

At eighteen, I thought my life would be different. I planned on marrying the girl next door, living by the ocean, and having a few children.

I did marry the girl, but then destiny screwed with my life, and I lost her.

It's been twenty-three years since I said I do. Less than twenty since the divorce and it feels like a lifetime since I let her go. She found happiness with another man. I'm no longer that teenager with dreams and an open heart.

All those moments I lived were so impactful they became a wound.

A wound so deep that I avoid certain things.

If I ever write a biography, I'd call it The Art of Avoidance.

I avoid relationships of any kind, settling down, and commitments.

I'm a drifter.

A ship that lost its anchor so long ago it keeps floating along the ocean. Well, more like flying around the world, but the result is the same. I visit my family, so they know I care about them, but I mostly keep my distance, so they don't suffocate me.

I just arrived from Zambia. It was an almost eighteen-month trip where I helped build a hospital. The moment I arrived in San Francisco, I texted the family group chat to let them know I'm back on US soil.

For how long? I don't know. It could be just a few days or maybe a few weeks.

No one bothers to respond immediately, but I'm not surprised that my phone rings while eating lunch. It's Kyle, my best friend and brother-in-law.

"Hi," I answer, setting my spoon on the napkin.

"Where are you? There's a lot of noise in the background." There's no hello, how are you, or… he's never been one to have a normal conversation.

"A coffee shop."

"City? What city? I couldn't find you with the fucking app. Did you change phones again?"

I sigh. If he could, he'd put a tracker on my ankle. My little sister gets anxious when she doesn't know where I am. She should focus on raising her five children and dealing with her husband. Kyle is too fucking needy.

"I'm in San Francisco."

"Huh, interesting."

"Is it? You know the place well, I'm sure there's nothing *interesting* here for you."

Kyle and I met in Santa Cruz, a town just an hour south of the Bay area. That's where I was born and raised. His family owned a vacation home, but he's part of the Maxwell family. The Maxwells are one of the wealthiest families in the state, maybe the country. I think his worst memories are buried somewhere downtown. He's better living in Evergreen, Colorado, far away from here.

"Don't play dumb," he snaps. "Why are you there and not here?"

"I'll visit you soon, honey. You know you're my one and only," I joke.

"Fuck you. My wife wants to know how long you're staying. She misses you—" He pauses long enough to make me want to hang up, but I don't. "We all miss you, Elliot."

Kyle used to be the clown of our friend group. He didn't care what happened around him, but now, he sounds more mature than I do. It's not like I haven't matured.

My sister, Cassandra, swears I have Peter Pan Syndrome, but I don't. There's a huge difference between not wanting to grow up and avoiding my past.

"How's Cassy? How are the kids?"

"You should come and visit us."

"I'll do it soon," I promise, though soon can mean six months or a year, or maybe even two.

I adore my brother and sisters, and sometimes I miss my best friends. However, they'll expect me to stay longer, and I don't like to stay in one place for too long.

"What are you up to?"

If I knew, I wouldn't be here, but I just say, "I'm still deciding."

It's not like a project is going to fall into my lap. Next week, I might make a few calls. "For now, I'm planning on taking it easy." I don't lie. I'm gently letting him know to fuck off.

"You can come and work for me."

I laugh. "No, but thank you for the offer." I'm tempted to tell him that we co-own his company, and we agreed I'd be a silent partner. Meaning, he runs it and makes monthly deposits into my account.

That's how I've been running my business affairs for the past six years—since Mom, my sister, Dahlia, and two of her daughters died in a car accident. I close my eyes, sending a silent prayer for their souls.

"Your sister would appreciate having you around for more than a weekend."

"Why don't I call you when I decide where I'm going next. Say hi to everyone for me."

"Elliot you—"

I cut off the conversation before it gets too heavy. I love my friend, but I'm not in the mood to discuss my future, my choices, or his nonsense. I go back to eating when I notice a woman holding a tray walking around the dining room as she looks for a place to sit and eat her food.

There's something about her that calls to me. Maybe it's her posture, those eyes, or the frustration etched on her forehead. She's beautiful but young. Too young. She could be my niece. Not many believe I have nephews and nieces who are in their early thirties.

If my niece Teagan were distraught, I'd love for someone to aid her. I rise from my seat and approach the frazzled-looking woman. "Would you like to share the table with me?"

She smiles, almost knocking me down to my knees. She's even more gorgeous than I thought a second ago. Her gray-blue eyes are big and bright. It's like staring at the ocean. I bet they're bluer when she's happy and look like a storm when she's angry.

This kid is too young, just walk away.

"I don't want to interrupt your meal," she says with a sweet, gravelly voice that hits me in the groin.

Okay, maybe I need to look for a woman who can take the edge off. It's been a long time since the last time I fucked someone. She's not the one though.

"Don't worry about me," I assure her, planning on just picking up my tray and leaving the place immediately.

"Okay, but it'll only take a few minutes. I'm a fast eater." She sets up the tray on my table, and I pull out the chair so she can sit. She glances at me, gifting me another smile. "Thank you. You're making me believe in humanity."

"Because you lost hope?" I ask, taking a seat. "Please, don't eat fast on my behalf. Take your time."

"I always eat fast."

"Why?"

"I grew up with six brothers. They'd scarf everything down. If I didn't match their pace, they'd leave me without dessert."

I can't help but laugh. "Six brothers, huh?"

"Yes, and a baby sister. We're a big family." She fixes the paper napkin on her lap, squeezes some hand sanitizer, and then grabs a spoon.

While she's eating, I study her. Brown hair with some auburn highlights, fine facial features, and her heart-shaped lips are tempting. She's pretty and probably too young. She might be just fresh out of college.

"You don't have to stop eating on my account," she says.

I shake my head, wondering what it is about her that hypnotizes me. Since we're sharing a meal, I extend my hand. "Elliot McPhee."

She smiles, meeting it. "Sorry, where are my manners? I'm Fern. My mind is all over the place today. People are just... not very nice."

I can't help but chuckle at her politeness. "Anything I can do to help?"

After a long yet soft exhale, she says, "If you can find a construction company that can take on my project, maybe?"

"There are plenty in this area. I doubt any of them will turn down a job."

"You'd think. I just finished a meeting with North Bay Construction company, and they shut me down when I said this is for a foundation, and I was hoping they'd donate—"

"Wait, you went to one of the biggest construction companies in the Bay area asking for a donation, and they rejected you?"

"Try biggest in the state," she corrects me with a smirk on her plumped lips. "And yes, I dared to ask them to work for me. Not that they let me say much."

"Biggest company on the West Coast, but that's not the point," I argue with humor in my voice. "What in the world did you ask for that they shut you down?"

She sighs. "I made the mistake of mentioning the words charity and donation. Even before I could pitch my project to them, they ushered me toward the exit. Which is weird because aren't construction companies supposed to woo their future clients?"

"Usually. Why did you flip the roles?"

"Who said it was my doing?"

"You." I grab a chip from the bag and munch on it as I consider offering my services. I know a lot about construction and spend most of my time doing volunteer work. We could help each other. "Why don't you tell me more about this project they rejected?"

She takes a bite of her sandwich. After chewing and swallowing, she explains, "I want a community with affordable housing close to the city. We have the lots, but before I can even tell the board what we're doing, I need to have an architect willing to design them, and a crew—"

Fern sighs in frustration.

"Take a deep breath. It seems like you have a big project on your hands, but you just haven't found the right person to manage it."

She grabs a napkin and wipes the corner of her lips and nods. "That's why I went to North Bay Construction. However, Jonathan Smith shut me down and invited me to get the eff out of the company."

Fern straightens her shoulders and tilts her head toward the door. "The CEO is an asshole. I swear he just agreed to see me because…"

She clamps her lips without finishing the sentence.

My jaw tenses. "Did he insult you?"

"He kicked me out of the building. He has quite a colloquial vocabulary. I bet if I had been there representing one of my brothers, he would've been trying to kiss my ass."

Some people are just entitled assholes. But maybe I should be thankful, because I could take on that project and give myself some time to think about where I'll be going next. It shouldn't take me long to draw up some blueprints and plan a community. I've done it a few times before.

"Why don't we finish our lunch, and I can follow you to your office. Then, you can tell me more, and I might be able to find the right person."

Her eyebrows draw together. "Just like that."

I shrug. "Why not?"

She laughs. "Sorry, who are you?"

"I thought I already introduced myself. The name is Elliot."

Fern can't stop the laughter. "Well, that should be plenty to trust you with this project. What are your qualifications?"

"Well, for starters, I know the right people for that kind of job." I wink at her.

She gives me a suspicious glance. "What do you know about construction?"

I show her my calloused hands. "Dad taught me from a young age so I could help him."

"Though that's helpful, I need more than a handyman."

This woman might want my résumé before I can even learn

more about the community. I sigh. "I've worked in construction for more than twenty years. I also have a degree in architecture and have a few engineer friends who might be able to give you a hand—for free. As long as your foundation is legit."

She's still not buying what I'm saying. I can see it in that doubtful gaze. "Are you pricey?"

"No, and if your cause is worthy, I might even donate my time."

"You don't have to. We can pay you, but—"

I point at her food, interrupting what might be her pitch. "Why don't we enjoy our lunch, and then you can proposition me. Maybe I'll even do a lap dance for free."

I wink at her, and her cheeks heat up.

Want More?

Accidental Pregnancy?

USA Today Bestselling author Claudia Burgoa brings you a fresh romantic comedy filled with an unexpected surprise, a wicked billionaire, and plenty of laughs.

The right life is the one you never see coming.

I had it all. The luxury apartment, hot dates, and the big office to go with long nights at the office.

Life was perfect.

But after a one-night stand, two little lines on a pregnancy test, and three lost legal cases later…

Well, overnight I went from career lawyer to single mom.

It's okay, I can do it. I'm ready to face this alone until…

Along comes Nathaniel Chadwick. Billionaire adrenaline junky. Everyone's favorite playboy… and my sister's brother-in-law.

He's as hot as he is jaded. When it comes to relationships and family, he'd rather jump off a cliff.

I wrote him off long ago, except since he learned about the baby he's been by my side.

Is it pregnancy hormones or is there something real happening between us?

I didn't expect any of this…most of all him.

***

Didn't Expect You is a billionaire romance of unexpected pregnancies, exciting encounters, and flirty love. It includes a very confused dog, a precious newborn, and a family you might want to belong to. This chick-lit novel is a romantic comedy with a HEA guaranteed!

Office Romance?

Billionaire Jackson Spearman is impatient, demanding, and private.

He's practically a recluse.

When his assistant goes on maternity leave, Amy Walker virtual assistant extraordinaire arrives to save the day.

Or does she?

Amy is inquisitive and far too optimistic.

She isn't impressed with Jackson at all.

They can't stand each other.

Unfortunately, they can't seem to resist each other, either. Soon, their work relationship starts to feel like something more…

Even when Amy meets her dream man, she can't seem to stop thinking about her annoying online boss.

And the woman who 's never fallen in love before, finds herself falling for two men.

Both of them have everything she's ever wanted.

But she has to choose one.

Can Jackson convince her that he can be everything that she needs?

Or will her past come back to haunt them and ruin her chance at love?

Lots of sibling banter and protective brothers?

USA Today **Bestselling author Claudia Burgoa presents a heartwarming, sexy romance about second chances and starting over.**

After a week off the grid, I finally get reception and the first voicemail I hear stuns me.

"You're summoned to Baker's Creek by the late William Tower Aldridge."

Twelve Years.

It's been twelve years since the last time I heard from the Aldridge family.

That one voicemail changes everything—I need the money the late William offers.

In exchange, I have to live eighteen months in Baker's Creek.

I've survived cancer, the jungle, and the plague.

This should be easy compared to all that, right?

Or so I think until…I see him.

Confident, charismatic, bitter, sexy as hell, Doctor Hayes Benjamin Aldrige.

My first love, my first kiss—my late husband's brother.

He hates me.

He still hasn't forgiven me for walking out on him, and I can't blame him. It's been over ten years, and I still have feelings for him.

But I faked it once and I can fake it twice.

I can survive eighteen months and that'll be the last time I see the Aldridge brothers.

Isn't it?

The Baker's Creek Billionaire Brothers series is a romantic comedy saga packed with the perfect mix of angst, tears, and laughs. If you like strong heroines & alpha males, steamy romances and witty love stories, this series is for you!

Thank you so much for reading ALONG CAME YOU.

I am so grateful that you picked up a copy of this book. If you're new to me, I hope this is the first of many stories we share.

Can you believe that we're on book 3?

Okay, that's a lie. I finished writing Caspian's book so technically, I'm on book four. I'm loving this branch of the Spearman family. If I didn't have a schedule, I'd be jumping onto the next book which is going to be just as amazing.

I know I said Gatsby was my favorite so far, but by now it's hard to pick any of them (Alex Spearman) kidding.

Elliot might not be a Spearman, but he's amazing all the same. When I wrote Perfect for Me (Scott and Hazel's story) my heart broke for him, because he deserved a happily ever after.

I'm so happy that after all this time, he found it and I can't think of anyone better for him that Fern (well, me, but I'm not available). But let's not digress.

I really hope that you loved Fern and Elliot's story as much as I did. I'll appreciate if you could leave a review on Goodreads, Bookbub, Amazon, and all other retailers. Also, if you love the Spearman family as much as I do, please spread the word about it among your friends.

Sending all my love,

Claudia xoxo

Acknowledgments

First and foremost, thank you to God because he's the one who allows me to be here and who gifts me the time, the creativity, and the tools to do what I love.

Thank you for all the blessings in my life.

Thank you to my family for your endless love and support.

Thank you to Dani and the team of Wildfire Marketing PR.

Hang Le, my longtime friend and my cover artist. She always understands what my books need.

Thank you to Wander Aguiar and Andrei for helping me find the image for this cover. It's always a pleasure to work with them.

Thank you to Gel for her amazing graphics and unlimited support.

Thank you to Caroline for her support and for taking the chance to be in Team Claudia.

To Yolanda, Patricia, and Melissa for always being there for me and for answering my nonsense.

Thank you to Amy R. for always going through the book and giving me new ideas and names.

To Amy, Mary, Bri, and Jenny for always listening to me while I'm writing.

Thank you to Chrisandra, Brandi, Darlene, Athena, and Dee for helping me shape this book.

To all my readers, I'm so grateful for you. Thank you so much for your love, your kindness, and your support. It's because of you that I can continue doing what I do. My amazing ARC team, girls you are an essential part of my team. Thank you for always being there for me. My Grammers, you rock! To my Chicas! Thank you so much for your continuous support and for being there for me every day! Thank you to all the bloggers who help me spread the word about my books. Thank you never cuts it just right, but I hope it's enough.

Thank you for everything. All my love,

Claudia xoxo

Claudia is an award-winning, *USA Today* bestselling author.

She writes alluring, thrilling stories about complicated women and the men who take their breaths away. Her books are the perfect blend of steamy and heart-felt, filled with emotional characters and explosive chemistry. Her writing takes readers to new heights, providing a variety of tears, laughs, and shocking moments that leave fans on the edge of their seats.

She lives in Denver, Colorado with her husband, her youngest two children, and three fluffy dogs.

When Claudia is not writing, you can find her reading, knitting, or just hanging out with her family. At nights, she likes to binge watches shows or movies with her equally geeky husband.

To find more about Claudia:
    website

Be sure to sign up for my newsletter where you'll receive news about upcoming releases, sneak previous, and also FREE books from other bestselling authors.

Made in the USA
Middletown, DE
05 September 2022